EYES OF THE SKULL

by
Philip Steele
and illustrated by Matthew Jeffery

HENDERSON
PUBLISHING PLC

©1996 HENDERSON PUBLISHING PLC

KEEP DOWN, keep pressed to the smooth rock. Don't breathe. There's just a few bushes of thorn between him and me. His brow is dyed blue and his eyes stare out from deep black rings. His fox-skin kilt is stained with dark blood. He stinks of blood and sweat.

HE IS LOOKING FOR ME, but it is I who should have spotted him. Wasn't it I, Kerak, who was given the honour of guarding Lookout Rock only a moon ago, in my thirteenth year, when I was made a warrior of my people? I still feel the pain from the razor-sharp bone that pierced my cheeks that night, but I wear the tattoos of my clan with pride. And what did the chief say to us? "Years of peace have made our people soft and lazy. It is up to you young warriors now to be alert and brave."

I FEEL SHAME... I have failed in my duty. I have let the enemy through our lines. What came over me? Was it this thundery heat that made me so drowsy? The shadows in the forest are so deep! A noise startled me and then I spied my enemy crawling through the dust like a snake.

His staring eyes have passed by my hiding place. I breathe in carefully. Suddenly he pulls himself to full height and raises a pole topped by a badger's skull, hung with tattered hide. He cups his other hand around his mouth and makes a yipping noise. Now more blue-heads appear over the brow of the hill, doubled over, grunting, moving in fits and starts. Keep calm. Keep counting. "One for an ash, two for an oak, three for a splash, four for a soak..." For pity's sake, now I'm reciting nursery rhymes like a baby – me, a warrior! My eyes sting with tears. Ten times ten. And ten times ten. Can THEY see ME?

Some carry heavy clubs, others have flint battle-axes, slings, savage knives and spears. This is no hunting party. This is a tribe in search of a home. In search of my home. Suddenly they are running down the gully under Lookout Rock, so close they must smell my fear. SO CLOSE!

Perhaps I can double back to the village. I twist round but a file of blue-heads is snaking down the back path. They surround me like a tide, I am helpless, I cannot move. Cold sweat pours down my neck. The attack has begun.

From the direction of the village I hear a long, high-pitched scream which curdles my blood. That is no pig being slaughtered, no yelping dog. That is the sound of my sister calling for me. Her cry seems to hang in this hot, close air. IT HANGS IN THE AIR FOREVER.

Chapter 1
In the News

"Open the back door, would you, Will?"

It was only nine in the morning but it was hot already. The downs above the village were lost in a haze and the air shimmered above Crickstone High Street.

Will's mum owned the newsagent's and her day had started early. There weren't just papers to sell. Lizzie Day's shop sold everything from sandwiches to videos.

"Oh, thank you Mr Bodgett. Hello, Jane! That's seventy five pence please." The off-to-work rush hour began. Will sat on the back steps and ignored the babble behind him. He tried to work out how many days it was until he had to go back to school. And how many days to his ninth birthday. And how many...

"Will! Give me a hand."

His mum needed help in the shop. Two large piles of the local weekly newspaper had just been delivered. Will cut the plastic tape that bound them with his penknife and piled them up next to the dailies. RAGE OVER NEW ROAD was the headline.

"I don't know what all the rage is about," said Jack Evans, leaning on the counter. "It'll mean much-needed work for folks round here. There'll be all kinds of jobs."

"But have you seen the route this motorway

link will take?" said another customer, studying the front page. "It'll cut right through the downs and through those beautiful old woods. It's a real shame!"

"The new motorway link will get us into Sheriton more quickly," said Mrs Neill.

"And to the supermarkets there," broke in Will's mum. "And do you know what that means? Loss of trade in the village. Do you remember how many shops there were here ten years ago? Well, there's just three of us left, now. If people can drive to the big stores in ten or fifteen minutes, it's the end of business for us."

"You're right there, Lizzie," said Jane Richardson. "And if you ask me, there's enough roads around here already! We'll get more heavy traffic through the village and more stinking exhaust fumes."

Will was thinking on different lines.

"Wow, there'll be diggers and trucks and huge bulldozers! Wicked! And they'll blast out loads of rock!"

"Will," said Lizzie, "you are not contributing to this debate!"

"I'm not what?" said Will.

"Scarper!" said his mum. "Go and tell your big sister to get out of her bed." She threw him the key to the side door.

"Boring!" sighed Will. He opened up the door and climbed up to the flat above the shop. "Cass! Mum says you must get up!" The radio was playing in her bedroom, but Cass wasn't

6

there. She wasn't in the bathroom either. "For once..." thought Will. He always claimed she spent at least twenty three hours a day locked in there, washing her hair or staring in the mirror. And she wasn't in the kitchen. She'd left a slice of burnt toast and half a cup of coffee on the table, though. And one of her silly magazines lay open on the table. How could she read such stuff?

Will went down into the shop.

"She's not there, mum. She's already up and out."

"Wonders never cease!" exclaimed Lizzie. "Well, do you think you could try to find her? I need to find out what her plans are for the weekend."

"She'll probably be off somewhere or other with Jay," said Will. "She spends all her time with him. It's not fair. She never does anything with me any more."

"But Jay's a nice lad," said Lizzie. "And she does care about you, you know. It's just that she's fourteen and you're only eight."

"I'm nearly nine!"

Will gave his mum the keys. He went out and got his bike from behind the shop. He practised some wheelies, skidding round in the gravel and kicking up dust. And then he remembered he was meant to be looking for his sister.

But Cass wasn't at Jay's house. Jay's mum, Rose Cunningham, wasn't there either. Will knew she was a nurse and had to work all sorts of hours at the hospital in Sheriton. Will did find Mr Cunningham though. He was working on his battered old car by the back garages, trying to fit a new radiator hose. And he was not in a good mood.

"Uh huh, Cass was here earlier. Jay was meant to be helping me with the car today, but the lazy so-and-so skived off. I think he and Cass went up on the downs."

Will paused and then asked one of those questions that drive grown-ups mad. "Mr Cunningham, why are hills called downs? They ought to be called ups. How can you go up on the downs?"

Ray Cunningham raised his head wearily – and banged it on the raised bonnet. "Ouch! Boy, boy, what nonsense are you on about now? Go and do something useful..." He rubbed his head.

Will rode off. He cut through a couple of alleys on the edge of the estate and crossed the playground. From here, a long chalk track led out of the village. It crossed a low bridge over the River Crick and then passed between electric fences, through green fields dotted with cows. The ditches along the track were high with big daisies and white cow parsley.

The ride was rough but Will's Trekster Zed bike was a winner. It was a bit battered, but it had loads of gears and super-tough tyres. After ten minutes, Will stopped to rest. The track split here. One path climbed steeply up the slope of the downs. The hillsides were bare, and there was no sign of Cass and Jay up there.

The second path curved away to the right. Here the hillside plunged into a deep fold, a valley carved out over millions of years by rainwater springs seeping through the chalk. At the upper rim of the fold was a great rounded dome of limestone – Lookout Rock, the kids called it. You could lie on the top of the rock and see the countryside for miles around. But if you lay down really flat, nobody could see you. It was a magic place.

Will had often cycled up to Lookout Rock with his friends, but for some reason he had always been scared to go much further. Not that he admitted it, even to himself. Only once had he dared to go down into the valley beyond, with his friend Connor – and they had gone deep into the woods. But then they had both suddenly run back to the open downs as fast as they could. They felt as if someone had been watching them down there...

The valley was a tangle of ancient forest. There were gigantic beeches and scrubby little oaks, not that Will knew all the tree names. The place just seemed very, very old. It smelt of musty fungus and rotten stumps. Parts of the wood were dark and gloomy. And there were holes in the undergrowth, damp, dark gullies which could swallow you up if you tripped on a bramble and fell. Some of them were just wild animal holes, the sets of badgers and the dens of foxes. But some of them were dangerous shafts, leading deep into the hillside.

All sorts of creepy stories were told about Crickstone Woods. There were tales of witches and headless ghosts and of sudden changes in temperature that could not be explained. In the old days, Crickstone people used to say that little folk came down from the woods by night and swapped their own babies for those of the villagers. Changelings, they called them.

It was Cass who had told Will many of these tales – just to wind up her young brother. Once, when Will was smaller, he had run to his mum in tears over one particularly scary ghost story. Lizzie Day had held Will tight and told him that there was no truth in such tales. She herself couldn't believe that these superstitions were still half-believed by some folk in the village. They belonged in the Middle Ages! She had a sneaking suspicion that half of the stories had been invented by the landlord of the Crickstone Arms – to attract tourists with more money than sense to the area.

Will had none of these tales of terror on his mind on this bright summer morning. But as he watched, a single cloud passed over the sun. Its shadow swept across the downs like a great bird of prey. It lingered for a moment over Lookout Rock. The valley darkened. It looked like an ugly frown on the face of the downs.

Chapter 2
Cass and Jay

Cass shivered as the cloud passed over Lookout Rock. She wished she'd put on something warmer than a thin T-shirt. But after a few minutes the sun came out again.

Far below in the village, a car windscreen reflected the dazzle and flashed through the haze. People used to signal to each other with mirrors, didn't they? It must have been a problem if the sun didn't shine for months on end... Thank heavens for the telephone. Cass loved talking to her friends on the phone, as her mother knew to her cost. Lizzie's phone bills had risen dramatically over the last year. It was Cass who had rung Jay this morning, suggesting a walk on the downs.

Cass loved it up here, high above the world. She was sitting cross-legged on the rock, plaiting a bracelet from scarlet and yellow thread. She would give it to Jay. Look at him now, the idiot, lying on his back staring at the sky. She loved the way he sprawled. And the funny things he said.

"What's up there, Jay?"

"Down there, Cass!"

"What?"

"Down, I'm looking down into the sky! It's just as well I'm stuck to the Earth by gravity, or else I'd fall off into endless space. I'm like a fly upside down on the ceiling. I'm looking into the depths of the ocean and its deep, deep blue! With white bits, like foam..."

"Jay..."

"Yes, Cass?"

"Why do you speak such totally terminal trash?"

"Because I'm a poet, you flaming flea-brain!"

Cass giggled.

"Then make up a poem for me, genius..."

Jay sprang to his feet and raised his arms, silhouetted against the sky.

"There once was a redhead called Cass,

A cool and a critical lass...

She went to the wood and – er – came to no good...

And... oh no, here comes trouble..."

Trouble came in the form of Will, red in the face, wheeling his bike down the path.

"Hi, Cass..."

"What do you want, bro? Can't I escape from my family for five minutes?"

"No," said Will firmly. "You can't. Mum wants to see you."

"Why?"

"Don't ask me. Hi, Jay. Hey, you two, did you hear about the new road? It's going to come right through here, over the downs and through the woods. It's all in the paper. Everyone in the shop was complaining. But I think it's great! They'll blow Lookout Rock to bits and shift a zillion tonnes of rock, the article says."

Jay picked up a pebble and hurled it over the edge of the rock. It curved through the air and tumbled into the trees, bouncing off a branch.

"Great," said Jay, looking out over the wood. "Crickstone enters the modern world. About time too!"

Cass scowled. "Hey, Mr so-called Poet. Haven't you got any FEELINGS? This place is magic! What about all those amazing wild flowers, you know, orchids, harebells or whatever? Some of them are meant to be quite rare! What about the owls that nest down there? Crickstone Woods haven't been touched since the Stone Age, for heaven's sake. Jay, a new motorway will destroy all that – and for what? Just so a few people can get to work five minutes earlier!"

Jay was irritated. "Well, I don't know about you, but I'm fed up with living in the sticks. No youth club, no action, no cool people. Just because your family's lived round here since the Stone Age, you think that nothing should ever change. Well I'm for progress. And if that means chopping down that spooky old wood, good riddance!"

Will interrupted. "You know how everyone says there are ghosts in the wood? Do you think it's true? Like that story you told me, Cass?"

Both Cass and Jay completely ignored him, glowering at each other. They hadn't had an argument before.

Both teenagers had been born in Crickstone,

14

had been to the same primary school and had both gone on to the high school in Sheriton. But a few people in the village still saw the Cunninghams as newcomers, even though the family had lived in the village for more than twenty years. Cass thought that must be because the Cunninghams were black. And that really annoyed her. How could people be so narrow-minded? Jay was as much part of Crickstone as she was. She knew that the attitude of some villagers hurt Jay, even if he never said so.

But now she was cross that Jay seemed to be lumping her in with those same villagers, the ones who lived in a rut and couldn't see that the world was changing. It wasn't that Cass was against progress. It was just that she wasn't sure that building a new motorway was progress.

Anyway, it went deeper than that. Cass had always felt some strange bond with the downs, with Lookout Rock and with Crickstone Woods. It was something she couldn't explain. She seemed to belong up here. Perhaps she had really been a changeling, one of those mysterious babies left by the little people on a Crickstone doorstep! She smiled to herself... But her feeling for the downs and the wood was deep inside her and it was real.

Cass decided she would do everything in her power to stop the road. And if Jay didn't want to get involved, tough. They trudged down the track, not speaking, Will following with his bike. As the three of them reached the end of the track, they noticed men at work in Horton's Field. They were fencing off areas with barbed wire and putting up metal signs: WORKS TRAFFIC ONLY, LORRIES TURNING, SECURITY PATROLLED. A hoist was unloading cabins from three big trucks.

Cass stopped in her tracks.

"Surely they can't be starting already? Hey, is all this going to be for the new motorway?" she asked a passing worker. Over his bare chest he wore a bright green safety waistcoat, with BZ CONSTRUCTION written on the back.

"This is going to be a supply depot," he replied, taking off his blue hard hat and mopping his brow with his handkerchief. "But this site is just the start. There'll be lots more. Now, you kids had better keep clear of here or you'll get run over."

A truck lurched over the rutted ground, its huge tyres kicking up a cloud of chalky dust.

"You're quite right," shouted Cass above the noise of the engine. "It is the start of something – something that will never happen!"

But the man had already turned his head away and was talking into a mobile phone.

"Come on, Cass," said Jay. "You're wasting your time here. Let's get back to the village." The two of them wandered back, but Will stayed behind, watching the vehicles arriving. Flatbed trucks carried in huge bulldozers, scrapers and graders. The hoists raised their heads like long-necked dinosaurs. It looked like the downs would never be the same again.

NEW INVADERS. Is there no end? Will my spirit never rest? Huge metal monsters are gathering on the edge of the wood. They snort and growl. What is happening to the world?

This time I must warn the gods of my people, this time I must do my duty.

My thoughts go back over and over again to that terrible day of the great battle. My death came with a strange, dream-like slowness. I turned to roll over when I saw a dark figure against the dazzling sun. The blue-head raised a taut bow and I saw the menace in his eyes. The gut string twanged. The arrow's feathers hissed through the air. A dull pain exploded in my head and the sun went red. The arrow pierced my eyeball. Sticky blood oozed down my cheek. A second arrow pierced my neck and all went dark.

The blue-head kicked my body over the edge of Lookout Rock with contempt and it rolled down the gully, deep into the ferns. My body soon rotted into the earth. Foxes scattered my bones. My skull was picked clean by the ravens.

BUT I COULD STILL SEE. I HAD NO EYELIDS TO CLOSE. I COULD NOT SLEEP THE SLEEP OF THE JUST. MY SPIRIT, TORTURED BY THE HORROR I HAD SEEN, COULD NOT REST. I WAS CONDEMNED TO STAY ON WATCH FOREVER. I could not rejoin my people, who lay slaughtered in the depths of the forest.

18

I have seen the seasons come and go. I have seen children playing and lovers laughing on Lookout Rock. And I have seen wave after wave of invaders. They cut back the great forest until it was just a pocket of woodland. They burned my trees for charcoal. Their sheep and goats ate my saplings.

Long after the blue-heads came the red-cloaks, the Romans. Grim-faced men who marched in straight lines... it was they who built the first road along the downs. And then came the men of metal, riders of horses who built the great stone fort called Crickstone Castle. They hunted in my woods, killing the boar and stag as we had done when I was alive. Later came the men who carried sticks of death, the guns that smoked and crackled and brought so many fine young men to their death. I wept for them as I had wept for my own people.

But none of the horrors I saw matched the terrible slaughter of that first day when the blue-heads came. The blood that soaked into the ground that day seemed to fix fear into this fold of the downs for eternity. Although I have no eyes, I have seen people shudder without ever knowing why. They run away screaming from these woods.

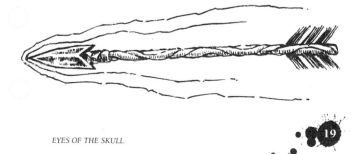

Chapter 3
The Policeman

Phil Sergeant was looking forward to retirement. His years in the police force hadn't been easy. But then he supposed that they hadn't been so tough either. Sheriton and district was not exactly downtown New York. Phil's patch was south of the downs, round Crickstone. No real problems there, just licences for moving farming animals, checking up on shotguns, a bit of sheep stealing, that sort of thing.

Phil blamed his problems on being born in the first place. Well, being born with a name like Sergeant. And never being promoted to the rank of sergeant after he joined the force. So all the lads in the nick called him Sarge, even though he wasn't one! You would have thought the joke would have worn thin after twenty five years, but it hadn't.

But now he was due for retirement, he didn't really care any more. The quiet life lay ahead... but not just yet it seemed. This morning the real sergeant, Hanway, stood in front of his desk looking like thunder.

"Tree houses!" barked Hanway. "What do they mean to you?"

Phil looked at him warily and swigged at a mug of grey-looking instant coffee. "Tree houses? Not a lot, Sarge. Is there a warrant out for Winnie the Pooh? Teddy Bears to be arrested for picnicking? The Babes in the Woods, guilty of trespassing?"

Hanway had no sense of humour. "They're building tree houses in Crickstone Woods."

"Who is and why and does it matter?"

"Who? A bunch of weirdos with clapped-out vans and dogs and tattoos and funny haircuts, that's who. Why? They're protesting about the motorway route, of course. And does it matter? Not yet, perhaps. But once they've built platforms in the trees we'll have the devil of a time getting them out when the contractors move in to cut down the wood. I want you to go and check them out. Okay, Sarge?"

"Yes, Sarge."

P.C. Sergeant enjoyed the drive over to Crickstone. It would be a lot quicker when the new road opened, it was true. But it would certainly spoil this fantastic view over the downs. Perhaps he felt just a twinge of sympathy with the protesters? Hanway would do his head in if he knew... Phil Sergeant drove into Crickstone and took a left through the housing estate. He would never forget that terrible day ten years ago when the kids here had stolen his patrol car. He had been the laughing stock of the county. SERGEANT WILL NEVER MAKE SERGEANT! said the headlines in the local newspaper. And he hadn't... All seemed quiet enough today, though. Past the church, out into the High Street.

A small knot of people was gathered by the clock tower, handing out leaflets. He parked the car and wandered over.

Wasn't that Lizzie Day's daughter, Cass? My, she'd grown up! What on earth was she doing?

"Sign the petition, stop the road! Sign the petition, stop the road!" Cass was pulling in the crowds, all right.

"Hello, officer. Are you going to sign our petition?"

Cheeky!

"Now, you are entitled to make a peaceful protest, Miss Day, but you mustn't collect money, or obstruct the pavement or the traffic. Do you understand?"

"Of course I understand. Stop the road! Sign our petition!"

Phil Sergeant shrugged his shoulders and walked on. The idealism of youth! They'd never stop the new road. He'd seen it all over the years, all the protests. They never made any difference.

He crossed the road and called in at Lizzie Day's shop. Lizzie was doing the stocktaking. She looked round.

"Can I help you? Is everything all right, Officer?"

"I hope so. I've just seen your daughter out there protesting about the road."

"So? She's not breaking the law, is she? I'm glad she's taking an interest in something serious, for once. My Cass isn't a kid any more, you know."

"Oh no, Mrs Day, I do understand." The policeman was taken aback by Lizzie's spirited defence of Cass. A lot of the parents he met would have been angry or indifferent. "It's just that all kinds of people seem to be getting involved in this protest, and it might turn rough. We wouldn't want your daughter getting into trouble, would we now?"

"Fair enough, Officer, I'll keep my eye on her." She smiled at him kindly. He grinned back. What a sensible woman, and nice with it. All on her own, too, or so he'd heard. Just like him, these days. He suddenly had a vision of a peaceful retirement from the force, a happy second marriage, helping Lizzie Day to run the newsagent's – and never seeing Sergeant Hanway's ugly face again. He smiled.

Hanway! He'd better get up to Crickstone Woods to check out Hanway's terrible tree-house dwellers! As he drove out of the village, he was surprised to see how the construction camp had already left its mark on the country-side, with rutted verges and soil and dust all over the road.

He turned the patrol car down a small flinty track and parked below the wood. High above, the sunlight caught Lookout Rock. He peered into the dappled shadows of the wood. Funny place, this. All very pretty to look at, but nature walks or rambles were not really his scene. Phil Sergeant was not exactly the outdoor type. He spent quite enough of his working life tramping the pavements without wanting to go for nature rambles on his days off!

The policeman began to feel a bit worried as he walked along the edge of the wood. Supposing these strange tree house people really were heavies. Supposing they turned on him? Better radio in his position now. Oh, he was sure he could handle them.

The footpath now entered the wood. In no time at all his way forward was blocked by Robin Hood and Maid Marian. Or so it seemed, except that Robin Hood had a stud in his nose and Maid Marian had a shaved head.

"Now then..." he began.

"We-will-take-you-to-our-leader," joked the girl, as if she was talking to an alien from Mars. Hanway had been right. Definitely a weird bunch of kids!

But he was even more surprised when their leader leaned over from the edge of a platform in the trees.

"Mrs Bodgett! Good heavens. I didn't expect to see you mixed up with this lot!" Mrs Bodgett from the village was... well, respectable. As respectable as they come. And not a day under seventy.

"With which 'lot', officer? These are my friends from the Feral Tribe and these are my friends from the village." She pointed to some more familiar faces from Crickstone. "And we all get on just splendidly."

P.C. Sergeant gulped. There they were, some of the most respectable people in Crickstone, hobnobbing with homeless travellers and city riff-raff – and all building platforms in the trees together, like a bunch of grown-up Cub Scouts!

He was offered a drink from a flask of hot tea.

"Well now, ladies and gents," he began. "We all have a right to peaceful protest, but I have to warn you that you may be breaking the laws of trespass."

"If the law allows this beautiful old wood to be cut down, then the law is an ass!" interrupted Mrs Bodgett.

"Right!" chorused the Feral Tribe.

P.C. Sergeant spilt his cup of tea. "I see," he said, feeling rather embarrassed.

"I wonder if you do," replied Robin Hood. "Because we ain't moving, see? Nothing will stop us, nothing!"

"Right," continued the policeman. "Well, I'm not here to take any action today, just to report on the situation to my senior officers. And to warn you that we'll be keeping an eye on things here. But I can tell you one thing. If you lot cause any damage to the wood or to the local farmland, you'll be in trouble. Now, I'd better be getting back to the station," said the policeman. "But I'll be back, you can be sure of that." He hoped he had been firm enough.

As he walked away, Phil Sergeant heard Mrs Bodgett's laugh echoing through the wood, like the neigh of a warhorse before battle.

"See you, policeman!" shouted Maid Marian.

As Phil drove back on to the road, he saw Cass Day crossing the fields to the woods. So, Lizzie obviously hadn't spoken to her. Or else she'd taken no notice. He did hope she wouldn't get into trouble. Still, the likes of Mrs Bodgett weren't exactly going to start a revolution. Were they?

☠

There are more and more monster-machines arriving every day. There are now many camps with cabins, surrounded by fences made of sharp spikes, rather like the thorn stockades we used to build around our village. Men in blue helmets swarm everywhere like busy ants. Blue-heads! Nothing changes. They dig trenches and lay down paths of small stones which they tip from great wheeled carts with flashing lights.

I FEEL THAT A MOMENT OF GREAT DANGER APPROACHES IN THE WOODS. IS THIS THE FINAL BATTLE? DO THESE PEOPLE NOT REALISE WHAT THEY ARE DESTROYING?

This is the last part of the Great Forest which once stretched all the way to the shores of the shining water. It is the last home of our gods, who have been sleeping throughout the long ages. These new invaders may not be wicked. But if they wake the Horned God or the Lady of the Waters-beneath-the-Earth... if they once arouse their anger... THEN THEY WILL UNLEASH FORCES THAT WILL MAKE ALL THE WARS BETWEEN MY LIFETIME AND THEIRS SEEM LIKE CHILD'S PLAY.

And yet defenders of the ancient ways have also come to the woods in the last few days. Some look like members of my own long-lost tribe, although their skins are marked with the tattoos of strange clans I have never seen before. They are building huts amongst the branches of the trees. They mean well.

Amongst them is a laughing girl with red hair. They call her Cass. I have seen her before, sitting in the sun on Lookout Rock, with the young black-skinned warrior. But I have seen this girl long, long before that. I have seen her in the days when the world was young, when I was alive. I have seen her gathering berries to make dye. I have seen her carrying fish from the stream, her red hair shining in the sun. She was my sister, Cass. She IS my sister. SHE DIED AND NOW SHE LIVES AGAIN...

Chapter 4
Kissing Death

The weeks passed by and soon it would be the end of the school holidays. This was the hottest summer since records began – and that was official, according to the local paper. There was good news for the Cunninghams, too. Jay's dad had got work as a security guard at the works depot for the motorway. It was hard sorting out the shifts, with Jay's mum working at the hospital. At the moment he was on nights. But the extra money would be welcome.

"Next summer, we'll take a holiday," said Jay's dad, " – Blackpool!"

"No, Italy!" chipped in Jay's mum.

"St Lucia!" laughed Jay. His mum and dad were glad to see him laughing. During the last weeks their son had been mooching around the house looking really fed up. He no longer saw that red-headed girl, Cass. And that seemed to be the problem. Not that he'd talk about it to anyone.

"Oh, he's still young," his mum had exclaimed.

"That doesn't make it any easier for him," his dad had sighed.

There was a reason Jay never saw Cass any more. Apparently she was always hanging out with the tree people, the protesters in Crickstone Wood. At least that's where young Will said she was. Jay was actually jealous, although he would have been the last to admit it. Why would anyone want to hang out with those creeps? The new motorway was bringing work to his family, and that was the beginning and end of the matter.

The road protest had divided the village. It had even divided families. Jay had laughed himself silly on hearing how Mr Bodgett had reacted to the news that his wife had joined the tree people. Bodgett, who had been a magistrate until he retired, had turned purple with rage. "The daft old buzzard! She's made fools of us all," he had exploded. And the old geezer had avoided Lizzie's shop ever since...

Anyway, today Jay decided to go fishing. "Time to relax," he muttered as he collected his rod from the hall and headed out for the pools below Crickstone Wood. Boy, the weather was close. His head ached. Was this the end of the heatwave? The clouds were building up into great towers above the downs.

As he left the High Street behind, he was surprised to hear the whoop of a police siren. A common enough event in Sheriton, but here in sleepy Crickstone the peace was seldom disturbed. One patrol car shot by at speed, headlights on, then another, then a large van. It looked like they were heading for the downs. What was going on? He hurried off in the direction of Horton's Field. But at the end of the track, a police motorcyclist had blocked off access to the public. A small crowd from the village was already gathering there to find out what was going on. Jay spotted Will on his bike.

"The contractors have started to cut down the wood!" said Will excitedly. "Can you hear the chain saws? And the protesters have chained themselves to their tree houses! Over there on the edge of the wood. They say they won't leave!"

"Cass! Is Cass with them?" Jay asked anxiously.

"I don't know. But that's the crew she's been hanging out with!"

Jay dropped his fishing gear and began to run across the field to the edge of the wood.

"Hey, you there! Stop!" It was P.C. Sergeant, mopping his brow in confusion. He didn't know where to turn next, for suddenly people were running everywhere. The first battle for Crickstone Wood had begun.

Jay slipped past him, and plunged into the undergrowth. The policeman shouted and came after him, but a root caught at his leg. Phil Sergeant hit the ground with a crash and a sharp pain spread from his ankle. As he tried to get up, the heavens opened. Raindrops drummed into the ground. A great flash of lightning tore across the sky and then thunder exploded like a bomb in his eardrums.

The contractors swore as newly excavated trenches filled with bubbling rain water and the ground churned up into thick mud. Everybody was skidding and sliding. Soon protesters and police and security men were wrestling in the puddles. It was hard to tell which was which.

There was still the whine of chain saws further along the edge of the wood. But now a rhythmic chant rose above it. "No road, no road, no road..." The sky darkened. Another great flash of lightning, another shattering crash of thunder. Blue police lights flashed across the field as more cars appeared.

Jay could hear Cass' voice amongst those in the chant.

"No road! No road! No road!"

And above the dull sound rose Mrs Bodgett's shrill voice: "We shall not be moved! Stand firm!"

What happened next, Jay never fully understood. It was as if a vast, dark shape launched itself towards him from a thicket in the wood. It had huge, spreading horns or antlers. Jay could have sworn that it was some kind of giant stag, bigger than any known in modern times, and that its eyes flashed red sparks through the gloom.

"Wha –?" yelled Jay. But the hellish animal knocked him into the ground before bounding off into the storm.

☠

Cass had taken up her position in the woods, below Lookout Rock. She was excited. And scared. The crowd of protesters in the wood had grown in recent days and she had spent more and more time with them. Her mum had told her not to get involved, but she couldn't help it. This action was really, really important. She had really got to know the woods well. She felt at home in its ancient ferny hollows. And at peace. All this made sense to her.

The contractors had moved in so suddenly on this sullen, sultry afternoon, hoping to take the protesters by surprise. The word of warning had been quickly passed down the line and soon the moan of chain saws had been heard in the distance. Some of her new friends had chained themselves to the branches, whilst others had sung or booed the contractors in their blue hard hats. It had all seemed good fun. At first.

Cass had felt for some time that a storm was coming, for a strange electric tingling arose from her spine. And then the storm had hurled itself out of the sky. This was not just the end of summer. It was more like the end of the world.

Mrs Bodgett was agitated. "This is really not the place to be in a thunderstorm," she said.

But Cass didn't listen. Her eyes shone and her red hair was plastered against her forehead by the torrents of rain. She looked like a wild animal, part of this ancient woodland. "Kerak!" she suddenly screamed, without knowing why. "Kerak!"

At that moment there was another flash of lightning and a great clap of thunder. A man in a blue hard hat ran to grab her, but suddenly he bellowed in pain as he was knocked backwards by a great charge of electricity. Cass gasped and ran forward, meaning to help him, but stumbled on a hard, round flint.

Down she fell, down into a newly excavated trench. Her head hit the edge of an excavator bucket with a nasty crack. Down, down into darkness. Her fall lasted just a couple of seconds, but she felt as if she was flying through the air for thousands of years.

And before the darkness closed in on her, another searing blast of lightning lit up an object in the trench, a sight she would never forget in all her days, a sight that burned itself on to her brain. It was a pale skull, with gaping black eye sockets and ancient, soil-stained teeth. And as she fell, it seemed that the skull came towards her and kissed her in a death-like embrace.

Chapter 5
In Casualty

As evening fell, the rain set in for good. The afternoon's deluge had turned into a steady drizzle. The thunder gradually rolled away over the downs and became silent.

The protesters were left in possession of their tree houses, shivering and soaked. They watched the contractors drive away and then fixed up tarpaulins to give themselves some shelter. People began to drop down from the branches to the ground. Some people lit small fires. There was no way a spark could cause damage on an evening like this. They huddled together for warmth as it became dark.

The protesters had won the first battle. Or rather the foul weather had won the battle for them. But they all realised that this war would be a long one. And nobody felt too cheerful.

Ten people had been arrested, including the fearless Mrs Bodgett. There had been so many needless casualties, too. One protester had broken his leg in a nasty fall from a tree. One of the company men had been trapped under a branch he had felled himself, and hurt his back. And nobody had been able to revive that worker who had been struck by lightning. Everyone prayed he wasn't dead...

The eerie wailing of the ambulances seemed to echo around the wood long after they had lurched across the field and sped away towards Sheriton.

The sound of the ambulances was the first thing Jay heard when he woke up. He had been out cold. Now he pulled himself to his feet, sore but not apparently injured. He tried to figure out what had happened. His last memory had been of what, a deer? A giant stag with great horns? Was he going soft in the head, or what? Cass! What had become of Cass? He limped over to the protesters standing around the nearest campfire. He was still wearing only a T-shirt, which was now plastered with mud.

"Are you all right, friend? You look awful! Come in by the fire!"

"I'm fine," muttered Jay, "fine. Look, have any of you seen Cass? A red-headed girl from the village? Cass Day?"

An uneasy silence fell on the group.

"Cass? Are you a friend of hers?" A woman wrapped in a blanket stepped forward. One of those Feral Tribe weirdos.

"Of course I am," said Jay with rising impatience. "Yes! I'm her best friend! Tell me what's happened to her!"

"She had a really bad fall into one of the trenches, man."

"Is she okay?"

"She seemed to bang her head as she fell. She was only half conscious and was moaning and crying. But she's in good hands..." added the woman hurriedly, seeing the worried look in Jay's eyes. "She was lucky, really. The guy in front of her – the one from BZ Construction – he was struck by lightning!"

"WHAAT?" cried Jay.

"Hey, hey – it'll be okay, don't worry, friend. Cass will be tucked up in a nice warm hospital bed by now."

But Jay was already haring across the fields. He had to get to Sheriton Hospital. His mum would be on ward duty by now. And his dad would already be on his way to the contractors' depot for the night shift, so there was no chance of a lift into town from him. He sprinted to the village, where he could already see the lights of the evening bus to Sheriton.

☠

At Sheriton Hospital, P.C. Sergeant was being wheeled out of X-ray. It was a sprain, not a fracture, apparently. Thank heavens for small mercies!

But what a shambles the whole operation had been. Sergeant Hanway would be seething. So many injuries, and one contractor dead, struck by lightning! A nurse had told him the terrible news.

And of course the press would be on to the story, by now. The last thing a hospital needed during an emergency was journalists jamming the switchboard and television crews hanging around like vultures. And those vultures would soon be asking the police awkward questions, too. Like why the force had failed to keep the situation under control. P.C. Sergeant winced as another sharp pain shot up his leg.

A woman was waiting in the corridor, white with anxiety. A nurse had her arm around her. He turned his head.

"Mrs Day! Lizzie!" What on earth was she doing here?

Cass' mum looked at the policeman blankly. "Oh...oh, it's you...yes, you! I should have listened to your advice, Officer. My daughter did get into trouble, real trouble. I'm not allowed in to see her yet, she's so poorly... it's all my fault, I should have kept an eye on her."

A tear ran down Lizzie's face. Phil Sergeant's own problems suddenly seemed very unimportant indeed.

"Oh, Mrs Day – Lizzie," he burst out, "don't blame yourself. Kids will be kids. She'll be all right. I'm so sorry! If I can be of any help..."

For a moment Cass' mother paused, surprised by the real warmth and concern in the policeman's voice. But then she was taken away into a small waiting room.

It was another hour before Lizzie got to see her daughter. Cass was in a special room, with a monitor recording her heartbeat. The light was low and the girl's face looked as white as a sheet, except for a dark bruise and nasty cut on her temple. Her eyes were closed but her lips were trembling. Occasionally she mouthed feverish, nightmarish words, little more than mutters and groans.

Lizzie held Cass' hand, which was cold as ice. She strained to listen. The words made little sense. "The skull!" she was moaning, over and over again. And then words in some strange foreign language. One sound kept repeating itself. "Kerak, Kerak, Kerak."

Terrible thoughts passed through Lizzie's head. Would Cass ever speak sense again? Or would she live in a coma for the rest of her days? Would she live at all?

Lizzie's mind turned to Will. She had left him at a neighbour's house, and hoped he was all right. Sometimes all the responsibilities of being a parent were more than she could bear. The clock on the wall seemed to be turning more and more slowly. At some point a nurse came in and, despite Lizzie's exhaustion, she recognised the woman as Jay's mum. The two women hugged each other silently.

"It'll be a day or two before we know if Cass'll be all right," said Mrs Cunningham. "We're all praying for her. Jay has been here for hours. He came over as soon as he found out..."

"Jay is here in the hospital?"

"Sure," replied the nurse. "But I didn't want him to disturb you. This is a time for family only."

Lizzie stared at her, thoughtfully. "Mrs Cunningham, Jay is family in a way," she said. "I feel sure Cass would like him to be here, you know. It might help."

So Jay was allowed in. He didn't know what to say to Mrs Day, and he said nothing at all to his mum. He looked at them both anxiously and then gently touched Cass' red hair on the pillow. He pulled up a chair and sat on it the wrong way round, facing the backrest. His chin rested on his folded arms. He stared and stared at Cass – until at last he slumped forward and fell asleep.

Chapter 6
Time Loops

There was a poem from the First World War which Cass and Jay had studied at school during the summer term. Their teacher had explained that it was written by an English poet called Wilfred Owen, who had died at the end of the war, in 1918. One of the millions. The poem was about the terrible waste of life in war, and it started:

"It seemed that out of battle I escaped
Down some profound dull tunnel..."

Jay had loved the poem. But it was Cass who was now living it out, floating down some deep grey tunnel into the past – or was it the future?

She heard snatches of tunes, of pipes and of dull war drums which throbbed like the beating of her heart. She saw blue-painted warriors swarming over the downs. She saw blood-soaked turf, crawling with flies. She heard women making a high, wailing noise. They were carrying dead bodies through the forest. At one point she looked down at someone who seemed to look just like herself, searching for something or someone. She saw a skull entangled in the roots of an oak.

Cass flew like an angel on a Christmas card. She crossed over rivers and plains, her red hair streaming out behind her. But she wasn't scared, she felt strangely at peace. Seasons flashed by, countless springs, summers, autumns and winters. They merged and flowed like the shadows of clouds passing over the grass. There was a wind, a high wind, but she couldn't hear it howling or moaning.

And then the wind dropped and Cass seemed to be sitting on Lookout Rock, one day in late summer. The rock was the same as ever, warm in the sunshine. But the view had changed completely. The woods she knew so well were now a great forest of oak and beech, stretching as far as the eye could see. Only a few narrow tracks ran between the trees and along the chalky tops of the downs. There was no sign of the village, no houses, no roads, not even any fields or barns.

Again, Cass did not panic. In fact, she felt that this was how it ought to look. She felt she was at home. A wisp of smoke rose from the deep woods beneath the rock. What was she wearing? Some long tunic, which she knew she had woven herself and dyed with blueberries. She pulled back her long red curls and secured them with a long pin of white bone.

A young freckled lad, red-haired like her and with tattoos on his cheeks, came running up the path to the rock. He carried a reed basket full of fish. He placed it on the turf and held out his arms, laughing.

MY TIME IS NEAR, MY TIME IN THIS WORLD IS COMING TO AN END. AT LAST.

The gods have sent my sister back to me. Here is Cass once again, the real Cass, sitting on Lookout Rock. She is so beautiful.

And here am I, returned to being a creature of flesh and blood, with real eyes in my head and the warmth of the sun on my arms. What time is this? Am I alive or dead? Has the great battle taken place yet or hasn't it? All I know is I have been spearing fish in the pools near the flint mine. It is just a normal day, as it was before the blue-heads came. Our village miners are still digging and delving, hacking out flints from the chalk with their picks made from the horny antler of deer. My father is repairing the timbers of our roof. It is as if nothing has happened. But I know that it will. I cannot make or unmake these things.

Time seems to loop and twist and turn like a maze, like the tattoos on my cheek. I hold Cass in my arms and kiss her on the forehead. She has returned to bring me peace.

"Kerak!" cried Cass, no longer knowing quite who she was, or even caring any more.

"Cass, I greet you!" The young warrior spoke a strange, lilting language, but Cass understood by instinct every word that he said. "We have both travelled far. We both know that great wrongs will be done in this place. We can do nothing about that, it is a mystery that only the Horned One knows."

"That is so, Kerak," said Cass gravely, speaking his language with a strange ease. "We cannot change the course of time. But I too serve a holy one, our Lady of the Waters-Beneath-the-Earth. And she has sent me back from the years to come to bring you peace."

"Why should she honour me in this way?"

"I do not understand her mysteries. Perhaps you have by now paid for your sins. Perhaps she wishes to clear the way for a greater battle – a battle to save the Earth itself and its ancient, wild places..."

"What am I to do?"

"You must tell me the secrets that were told to you when you became a man, when you received your tattoos. You must tell me how to find the secret place of the Horned God, where our warriors are buried. And you must recite to me the spells to be spoken at the end of time."

Kerak reddened and turned away angrily.

"You know I am forbidden to tell you these things. You are a girl. I am honour-bound to keep these things secret."

Cass put her hand on his shoulder. "Kerak, I do know you have to be loyal. Oaths are not easily broken. But you have to tell me these things if all is to be well – with you, with our lands and our gods in the years to come. For that is where I must return to make all well. The scars must be healed."

"How do I know you are not some witch, pretending to look like my sister, sent to trick me?"

"You don't," replied Cass. "You must trust me."

Kerak bit his lip and stared out across the forest. And then after a long silence, he turned to Cass.

"Very well. These are the things you must know... The Horned God appears amongst us in times of trouble as a leaping stag with burning eyes. His dwelling place lies wet but dry, high but low, amongst the oak roots but amongst the clouds... To approach his dwelling you must become a fish, a mole, a spider, a fly. Our brave warriors sleep in his dark halls until the end of time. The spells to be spoken at the end of time are as follows..."

Kerak broke into a long, low chant. He stumbled at first, but then the verses he had learned from the holy man of his tribe came rolling from his tongue. Cass stopped him from time to time, repeating lines and checking them. It seemed like hours that they were together, but it might just as well have been minutes or seconds or centuries. And as Kerak recited the spells, it seemed that the sun grew paler and paler and the sky became silvery grey. The outlines of the two figures on the rock began to grow faint and they eventually disappeared into mist.

☠

44

EYES OF THE SKULL

Lizzie Day came back to the hospital with Will during afternoon visiting hours the following day. Mrs Neill was minding the shop. Will was surprisingly quiet for once. Even he seemed to realise the seriousness of the situation.

"I think the worst is over now," said Mrs Cunningham, her hand on Cass' brow. "Her temperature has come down and she's breathing more easily. I dressed the head wound again just before you arrived and it looked a lot better."

"What are her chances, really?" whispered Lizzie Day anxiously.

"We won't know for several days," replied the nurse, "but the doctors say they are pleased with her progress. It's my guess she'll be fine. It will be a long time before she's back to her old self, though, you must understand that. She will have to take it very easy. And I'll make sure that my Jay doesn't keep on pestering her."

"Don't you worry about your son," said Lizzie. "He has shown himself to be a real friend. How many hours was he here last night?"

"Too many! But you're right, he does mean well."

The pale afternoon sun streamed in through the window.

"Mum? Will?" Cass' voice was a whisper. Lizzie bent over her daughter's bed as Cass' eyes opened sleepily. "Mum, don't worry, everything will be all right..."

"Sssh, darling, get some sleep now," said Lizzie with relief.

It was only as she was leaving the hospital entrance half an hour later that it struck her. Wasn't that a little odd? Surely it was she who should have been telling Cass that everything would be all right, not the other way round...?

Chapter 7
Back to Reality

The summer was fading fast and there was already a chill in the evening air. The protesters were still in their tree houses and the road contractors were still busy, although they had postponed any further tree felling in Crickstone Wood for the time being. The contractors were determined to go ahead with the scheme, but after that first night they were acting more carefully. There was talk of legal action to stop the road going ahead. After the protest, Mrs Bodgett had appeared in court and been bound over to keep the peace – much to the embarrassment of her husband, who now regarded her as a traitor to her country, somewhat worse than Guy Fawkes himself.

Cass had come home and was allowed up during the day, although she tired quickly and had to go to bed early. Term had started, but the doctor reckoned it would probably be half-term before Cass would be well enough to attend classes again.

Cass' mum had forbidden her to go back to the protesters in the wood. Still, she had become quite a local celebrity, with her photo in the papers. Some people said she had been very brave in putting her ideals into practice. Others said that she and young people like her were a disgrace to the village. But more and more people were now signing the petition against the road and were wearing badges and T-shirts calling for the road to be stopped.

One good thing, Cass was friends with Jay again. They didn't even argue about the road. Cass realised that Jay was now in a difficult position, with his father working as a security guard on the site. Jay just came around every now and then after school. He brought tapes he had recorded for her, and once he brought her an amazing book of poetry.

One Saturday afternoon, Cass was sitting in the kitchen drinking a cold coke she had taken from the fridge. Jay was standing by the window, absent-mindedly watching Will wearing out the brakes on his bike. Cass was doodling on the back of the local paper.

As Jay came to stand behind her, she heard a quick intake of breath.

"What's that?" snapped Jay.

"It's the Horned Go – it's a stag," said Cass, puzzled for a moment over her slip of the tongue.

"I've seen it!" said Jay.

"You've seen a stag?"

"No, I've seen that stag," said Jay.

Cass turned round and stared at him.

"When?"

"On the day you were injured in the woods. I realised you were in the thick of the trouble and I was running to help you. That hulking great beast leapt out of the shadows in the wood and knocked me stupid. Or at least that was what I imagined."

"The Horned God appears amongst us in times of trouble as a leaping stag with burning eyes," said Cass.

"You what?" Jay wrinkled his forehead.

"What did I just say?" muttered Cass. "I'm so confused! Oh Jay, something happened to me while I was in the hospital. A dream, I suppose. But it did seem incredibly real."

Jay pulled up a chair and put his elbows on the table. "Okay kiddo, tell your uncle Jay all about it."

"You won't laugh at me?"

Jay looked at her levelly. "I'm not laughing, Cass. I've just seen you draw a picture of my dream. Now you can tell me about yours."

"Well..." Cass paused and fiddled with a strand of her hair, as she often did when she was thinking hard. "I'm sure I saw a skull as I fell into the trench. It came out of the darkness and... and it kissed me."

"You were kissed by a skull?"

"You're laughing at me, now!"

"I'm not!"

"Well, after that it all turned really bizarre. It was like a video really. You know, rewind, pause, fast forward again. I went back in time Jay, it was like a whirlpool, or a tunnel. I went back to the time of some terrible, evil war up on the downs. A massacre. I knew it had happened long ago in the past but I knew at the same time that it was about to happen, in the future. It was like a – a sort of time loop. It must have been sometime in the Stone Age, I suppose, because there was forest everywhere, no Crickstone, no castle, no roads..." She looked at Jay warily, from under her fringe of red hair.

"Go on..."

"Jay, I belonged there. I was wearing the clothes, bone jewellery and flowers. They were my people."

"And you met Kerak?"

It was Cass' turn to look utterly amazed.

"How on earth did you know that?"

"I didn't. I heard you muttering the sound when I visited you in hospital. I was sure it was somebody's name. I was jealous!"

"Oh Jay, you shouldn't have been. Kerak is my brother. Was my brother. He was killed in a massacre, thousands of years ago, but he was never buried properly. His sister – that was me – his sister never found his body. Kerak has haunted Crickstone Wood and Lookout Rock, for thousands of years. Jay, it was his skull that I saw as I fell. I'm sure of it. Oh, I don't know. Was all this just a dream? Look, I really do believe I was sent back in time."

"But why?"

"To lay Kerak to rest. And to save the wood from the road building. Somehow the two things are connected, but I'm not quite sure how. Look, it seems that Kerak was a young warrior on lookout duty before the great battle took place. He failed to warn my tribe of the danger and was killed. But his spirit continued to keep watch, over the ages. And now he has to warn his warriors of the new danger which is about to happen. Why is the motorway scheme so important in the scheme of things? Because Crickstone Wood is the sleeping place of the old gods, the gods people worshipped before the Christians came. The Horned God, the great stag. The Lady-beneath-the-Waters. And if nothing is done, all the power of the ancient gods will be unleashed on our modern world. Jay, I really do believe that my spirit met Kerak's and that he told me the truth."

Jay remained silent, watching Cass. She looked pale and feverish again. He was afraid she was overdoing things. What a story! But it was obviously a crazy dream brought on by her injury. Wasn't it? After all, hadn't they been talking about the Stone Age just before the protest? And hadn't she already been worrying herself stupid about the wood, about the road building? She had spent too much time with all those weird hippies. Or been given too many pills in hospital. One bang on the head and...

"Jay, what are you thinking?" broke in Cass.

"Cass, you know you were very ill in hospital. It's hardly surprising you had all these nightmares in your head, all these skulls and massacres and whirlpools."

"Jay, you don't believe me, do you? Well then, how come you saw the stag, the Horned God?"

"Good point, Cass. I don't know. I just don't understand any of this!"

Cass' mum was shutting up the shop below. The alarm rang briefly as she switched it on and locked up. They heard her coming up the stairs.

"Cass, you look dreadful!" said Lizzie as she came into the kitchen. "It's time you were back in bed, my girl! Jay, shouldn't you be going home?"

"Yes, Mrs Day, Cass does seem a little... overtired."

While Lizzie called Will in for his tea, Cass whispered urgently to Jay.

"I can remember all the details that Kerak told me, Jay. I am sure I have been told enough clues to work out the hidden places of the gods and where I can find them and how I can bury Kerak and how I can stop the road..."

"Easy, Cass, easy."

"Jay, I'm still too weak. You must help me..."

"We'll talk. Get some sleep. I'll see you soon."

As Jay slipped out, it was a perfect evening. The downs were peaceful and the trees in Crickstone Wood were bathed in a yellow light. The real world! He drew a deep breath and wandered off in the general direction of the chip shop. Soggy chips in curry sauce seemed like the best possible treatment for an overdose of spookiness.

52

Chapter 8
Proof of the Past

It was official. There would be an appeal against the council's decision to allow a motorway across the downs. In the meantime, all work would be halted. The big boss at BZ Construction was furious at the delay. He ranted and raved on the television news. "Bureaucrats! Do-gooders! Luddites!"

"What's a Luddite, mum?" asked Cass, tucked up on the sofa.

"Someone who hates new technology and machinery, who stands in the way of progress."

"Huh!" snorted Cass. "Doesn't this man realise that half the road protesters are talking to each other on the Internet? He's the dinosaur, not us!"

But the appeal was going to happen, whether BZ liked it or not. It seemed that as the protest had gained more and more support over the last month, the politicians had been forced to sit up and take notice. And all sorts of experts had now stepped into the battle. There were geologists, archaeologists, speleologists, ecologists, meteorologists, botanists, civil engineers, herpetologists, ornithologists... There were planners and economists and accountants and barristers and councillors and Members of Parliament. Jay was beginning to think the BZ boss had a point! Too many boffins and bureaucrats...

But Cass, who was feeling much better, had been allowed by her mum to go along and sit in the public gallery for a day and listen to the planning decision being challenged. And as it was already the beginning of the half-term holiday, Cass had decided to drag Jay along with her. Just because it was the chance of a whole day out with Cass, Jay had agreed. The appeal was being held at the council buildings in Sheriton.

The two got off at the bus station. It was drizzling this morning and Jay stepped straight into a puddle. Cass pulled out her umbrella.

"Hey, get your spoke out of my eye!" cried Jay.

"Come underneath and get dry, you idiot!"

He put his arm round her and they walked up Market Street.

"Jay, you haven't forgotten what I said? About the skull and what we have to do?"

Jay shrugged his shoulders. "Nope."

"So will you help? We have to take some action."

"Look, Cass, it might not be necessary. Now the inquiry has been set up, the whole road scheme may be stopped anyway. If we get involved in all that spooky stuff, we're going to look like complete idiots."

Cass' eyes blazed in anger, so Jay quickly changed tack.

"Okay, okay. I promise that I'll help if I have to. But first of all, let's see what this appeal turns up."

There was a large crowd outside the council buildings. People held placards with hand-written slogans. Cass recognised a lot of them from the protest in the woods, the members of the Feral Tribe – and they recognised her.

"Hey, how are you, Cass?"

"Are you better, girl? Are you going to join us?"

Jay stood to one side, feeling rather left out of the reunion.

"I'm fine, now." Cass patted one of their dogs, a cute little terrier. "Jay and I were just going to go into the public gallery. We want to hear just what they're up to."

The bulky figure of Mrs Bodgett loomed forward out of the rain.

"Quite right, my dear. You get inside and keep dry. You've been very ill, I hear, and we don't want you catching double pneumonia."

The policeman on the door recognised Cass, too. P.C. Phil Sergeant was back on duty, cursing the rain and desperate for a hot cup of coffee.

"Hello, young lady."

"Oh, it's you."

"Are you better? I saw your mum at the hospital after the road protest, and she told me how badly you'd been injured. I sprained my ankle during that protest."

"Well, I'm sorry. But you shouldn't have been protecting the contractors, should you?"

"I'm not protecting anything but the law of

the land," started P.C. Sergeant, but Cass had already given him a withering look and swept through the doors, with Jay behind her.

The morning session of the inquiry was dull enough. There were endless reports to be presented and discussed. Jay fell asleep at one point and Cass had to nudge him awake. The council's chief planning officer gave them both the giggles. He kept taking off his glasses nervously and putting them on again.

"He has to be the most boring man in the world!" whispered Jay, and he started to count the number of "ers" and "umms" that the great man uttered. He gave up at one hundred and twenty.

But the afternoon session was different. A young woman called Linda Brookes was called. She was from the county's archaeological trust.

"I would like to point out that we originally applied for a permit to dig this site before the contractors moved in in August," she began, "and we were refused. But since then a trench dug by an excavator has laid bare what we believe to be a series of Neolithic post-holes."

"Would you care to explain what you mean in terms we can all understand?" interrupted the toad-like chairman, a touch drily.

"Of course. These holes were probably once filled with the timber posts of houses, fences and other structures. We believe that they belong to the late Stone Age."

Cass clutched Jay's hand and her eyes brightened with excitement.

"Yes!" she hissed in triumph. The archaeologist continued.

"Furthermore, we have carried out further studies in Crickstone Wood and the nearby downland. It seems to us that it is quite possible that these contain one of the largest Stone Age mines in western Europe." Jay, too, was now sitting up, listening to every word.

"Now if that were so, what would they have been mining for?" inquired the chairman. "Gold? Copper? Iron? Are you suggesting that modern mining companies might have an interest in the site?"

"Hardly," replied Linda Brookes curtly, "this was the Stone Age." There was laughter in the public gallery. "No, the villagers would have been mining flints for use as axe heads, arrow tips and knives. They dug the flints out of the chalk with picks made of antler horn and wood. The distribution of arrowheads found in this area over many years suggests that a large battle may once have taken place on this section of the downs, while a number of half-shaped flints suggests that they were being mined and flaked here over a long period as well."

Linda Brookes ended her speech with a demand that the road works should either be stopped, or at least postponed until the site had been examined properly.

"Come on, Jay, let's move!" whispered Cass.

They hurried out of the hall.

"Right. We're going to the public library."

Jay had given up asking questions. He too had been shaken by what he had just heard. So – there probably had been a Stone Age village in Crickstone Wood. And there may well have been a big battle there, too. Could Cass really have travelled back in time? In her mind, at least. Could she really be Kerak's sister, reborn at the end of the twentieth century?

"What are you looking at me like that for, Jay?" asked Cass.

"I think I'm beginning to believe your dream," he replied.

The rain had stopped. They ran across the street to the library. They had often been sent here from school to research class projects. Cass asked the librarian where she could find books on local history and archaeology. There wasn't much in the history section, but the librarian did find a small booklet called *Neolithic Artefacts recently discovered in Crickstone Wood*. Recently? It had been published by the Sheriton Museum in 1935.

"Wow, it's a piece of history itself!" joked Jay.

"Then treat it carefully," said the librarian.

They sat at the long table in the reference section and opened the book. The pages included many precise, measured drawings of flint scrapers and axe heads and arrowheads, of scraps of pottery, of polished stone beads and bone pins. Cass pored over them.

"Yes, yes," she grunted excitedly. "No, that one is wrongly labelled. It is a stone weight for a loom. For weaving cloth. I..." She looked up at Jay and he stared back at her, speechless.

She turned to the final page. There was a drawing of a strange pattern, a spiral maze that some local historian had found carved on a rock in the heart of the wood.

"Look at this! Jay, we must find this. These were the patterns tattooed on Kerak's cheeks. I think this maze could be the key..."

Cass stared at the lines, which swirled like snakes across the page, until her eyes lost their focus.

Chapter 9
Strange Sights

P.C. Sergeant entered the station, took off his helmet and hung up his rain-soaked coat. He went to make an instant coffee. The mugs by the electric kettle were a public health hazard, he decided. There ought to be laws against germs like those.

He sat down at the desk and wearily pulled over a pile of paperwork. Another hour and he'd be off shift. Home to a shower and perhaps a video and a pizza. Or would he finally dare to call in to see Lizzie Day? He'd need to think up some excuse. It was a pity her Cass had been a bit short with him this morning... Oh no! Hanway!

"Sarge!"

"Sarge?"

Hanway leaned on the filing cabinet, scratching his moustache.

"Everything okay at the hearing today?"

"Fine. Plenty of protesters, but all peaceful."

"Was our Mrs Bodgett behaving herself?"

"She was indeed."

"Pity. I'd like to see her ladyship get her comeuppance."

"Yeah, Sarge, I can see she really is public enemy number one," said Phil Sergeant sarcastically. "Anyway, I think things will stay quiet until the results of the inquiry are known."

"Well, I wouldn't count on it. The protesters are still out and about and spoiling for trouble. I want you to keep an eye on things."

"Right, Sarge!"

Sergeant Hanway wandered off, whistling out of tune. The man was so irritating! Phil Sergeant reached for a pen and worked his way through his report, underlining certain sections. He needed to follow up some details. He was just walking over to run a computer check, when the swing doors flew open and he collided with a high-speed, evil-smelling, foul-mouthed bundle of humanity.

"Hold on! Easy does it! What's all this then?"

The duty officer from the front desk came running in after the intruder and grabbed him firmly by the arm. Phil Sergeant stood back and gazed at the human cannonball.

"Oh, it's you, Jacko."

"Do you know this man, Sarge?" asked the desk officer. Did he know Jacko? Surely everyone in the county knew Jacko. He was a wizened old fellow who drank too much and slept rough, and who would regularly try to land himself in a nice warm police cell for a kip on a rainy night. And if it meant breaking a window to be taken in, then so be it. He was harmless enough, though, Phil Sergeant was sure of that.

"Yes, I know Jacko," said Phil. "How are you, old son?"

Jacko was in a state of great excitement, but

the words tumbling out of his mouth made little sense. The old man's face was white and drawn and his eyes were starting out of his head like big blue marbles. A dark bruise spread over his temple.

"I had to find you, but him on the door, he tried to throw me out. I tell you, I've n-n-never seen the likes of this in all my life. I - I..."

"Come and have a cup of tea and tell me all about it, Jacko," said Phil Sergeant. He raised his eyebrows to the duty officer. "It's okay, I'll handle this one."

The tea was warm and comforting, and old Jacko began to quieten down. "Well, I was wandering up Crickstone Wood way," he told Phil Sergeant. "Sober as a judge of course..."

Phil noted that Jacko stank of cheap sherry.

"What were you doing up there?" he asked.

"Well those young folk who live in the trees up there, they are gooduns, they give me a cup of soup from time to time, or a sandwich. So as I say, I went up there looking for company, only most of them weren't there, they'd all gone off into town for some reason. But I did find a bottle of booze hidden away in a tent up there -"

"Which you nicked," broke in the policeman.

"No! Well, I...er...borrowed it, you understand."

"Carry on," said Phil Sergeant.

"Anyway, I fell asleep, like. And when I woke up I was soaked to the bone. Well I thought I'd woke up, but I was still having nightmares, see. With my eyes wide open."

A look of genuine terror passed over the old tramp's face.

"And what did you see?"

"First of all a bleedin' great deer jumps out from the trees and crashes bang in to me. It kicks me in the forehead, here." He pointed to the bruise.

"Yes, there are still a few red deer around Crickstone."

"Nah, nah, you don't get my m-meaning. This was twice the size of any real deer, with eyes that burned right through me. It bellowed like a f-f-flaming f-foghorn."

"Okay, so it was a big deer. A stag. And this is the rutting season, when the red deer breed, right? The males are very aggressive and fight. You don't mess with them."

"But THEN the s-s-s-skull s-said it was the Horned God!"

Dear me, thought Phil Sergeant, the old boy really has pickled his brains today. He's off his rocker.

"What skull? Are you telling me you found a body up there?"

"Found a body? N-no! The s-s-skull found me! After I'd been knocked down. It was s-staring at me. With horrible black maggoty eyes. And its teeth was rattling in its jaw like dominoes. And it spoke to me in some funny language, but I could understand it like it spoke English."

"Uh huh. And just what did this skull say?"

"It said it had a message from the – the H-h-horned God. The message was that the final days had come. And that, I don't know, 'those who sought to destroy the woods would perish' or some such n-nonsense."

"Nonsense. You said it, Jacko." Phil Sergeant picked up the mugs of tea. "You'll have to try harder than that if you want a dry night in the cells."

To the policeman's surprise, Jacko clutched on to his sleeve, as if he really was scared out of his wits.

"I'm telling you the truth, guv," he protested in vain.

"Of course you are. Look, chummy, I'm going off duty now and I don't want to hang around here any longer, even if you do. I'll give you a lift over to the Sheriton Homeless Hostel if you like, it's on my way home."

Phil Sergeant slipped the old boy some money before he dropped him off. He felt depressed. What a miserable life people like Jacko had to lead. They should be cared for properly. But then, he wasn't too sure Jacko would ever let himself be looked after. On a sudden impulse, the policeman decided to drive over to Crickstone. Not to go to investigate severed heads or monster-sized deer, but to drop in on Lizzie Day!

It was Cass who opened the door twenty

minutes later. And her welcome was not very friendly.

"Look, are you following me around, or what? What do you want?"

"No, I'm not following you around. I'm not even on duty. And it's not you I've come to see. I wanted a chat with your mother."

Cass stared at him suspiciously.

"Who is it, dear?" called Lizzie down the stairs.

"Mrs Day, it's me – Phil Sergeant, Sheriton police station!" called out the policeman.

Lizzie came to the top of the stairs, holding a tea towel. "Well hello, how nice to see you. Won't you come on up? Cass, invite Mr Sergeant in."

Cass scowled. She showed the policeman into the living room and went off into her bedroom, slamming the door shut behind her. Will, who had been playing cards with her when the doorbell rang, pulled a face and followed her out of the room. Phil Sergeant felt rather nervous. This wasn't a very good start.

"I hope I'm not making a nuisance of myself, Lizzie. I'm not here on work, whatever Cass might think. I just wanted to call in and see how you were getting on."

"We're getting on fine. I'm sorry Cass was so sulky. She's been through a lot lately. She seemed to make a good recovery from the accident, but I'm still worried about her. She has something on her mind, I'm sure of it. She'll be back at school next week and I'm hoping that will sort her out again."

The two grown-ups chatted away. The policeman began to feel more at ease as Lizzie seemed genuinely interested in his work and what he had to say.

"You wouldn't believe some of the characters we have to deal with." He began to tell her about old Jacko and the strange things he had said.

Cass felt sure that the policeman was talking about her behind her back. So she tiptoed back into the corridor and put her ear to the living room door. Will followed her out, but she put her finger to her lips and frowned at him. And as she strained to catch the conversation, she heard more than she bargained for. "...Flaming great deer!... a message from the H-h-horned God..." The two adults were laughing out loud, but Cass felt like ice. This message was for real.

She went to the phone in the corridor and hurriedly punched in Jay's number.

"Come on. Come on." The phone was picked up at last. "Mrs Cunningham, may I speak to Jay?" A pause. Hurry up. At last. "Jay, Jay, can you come over here? Now? At once!"

Chapter 10
Moonlight Madness

Jay came over soon enough, and arrived just as the policeman was leaving the front door.

"It was good of you to call in Phil, thanks," said Cass' mum. "Oh, do you know Jay?"

"I believe we may have met somewhere," said Phil Sergeant, carefully avoiding any mention of a certain stormy afternoon not so long ago, when Jay had scrambled past him and run.

Good on you, thought Jay.

"Hi. I came to see Cass, actually."

"Well, I presumed that's why you were here. She's upstairs."

Jay bounded up the stairs.

"What was all that about? Why's the policeman here? Is there some trouble, Cass?"

"Oh, he's not the problem. He just came round to see Mum. Weird enough, eh? No, it's something he said to her that I overheard. Something totally amazing. Come through into the kitchen."

Her mum walked back into the room. "Wasn't that nice of Phil to call by? He's a good man, you know. Right, I'd better go and sort your brother out."

Cass sat Jay down in the kitchen, and in hushed tones began to explain what she had heard. Jay whistled.

"Wow! So this old drunk saw the Horned

God, just like I did!"

"And he saw the skull. Kerak's skull, I'm sure of it, Jay. And that has to mean that our time is running out. If the wood is harmed, heaven knows what powerful forces will be let loose. We must act *now*. We must find Kerak's skull and bury it in the secret place."

"Okay, but we must keep cool, Cass. We must plan our moves carefully. Step one: how do we find the skull?"

"Well, if I did see it as I fell, we must find the trench where the accident happened. It must still be there. After all, work won't start on the site again unless the council gives the go ahead."

"When will the appeal be over?"

"On Friday. The papers said they will come to a quick decision because it's just an appeal against a planning order that's already been passed. Anyway, we'll both be back at school next week. It's now or never, Jay. And we'd better keep it secret. Under the cover of darkness."

"Tomorrow night?"

"Tomorrow night. We'll get the skull and bring it back here. And then we'll try to work out where we have to bury it."

"Write down everything that Kerak said to you in your dream, Cass. Then we'll be able to finish this business for good!"

"And save the world?"

"And save the world, Cass! You bet." They both laughed, a little nervously. And he kissed her.

☠

The next evening, Cass met up with Jay behind the chip shop. Both were dressed as if for a commando raid. Thick sweaters, hooded jackets, scarfs, black jeans and trainers, small backpacks. It should only take a couple of hours, and they would be back before their parents knew a thing.

It was a chilly autumn night. Their breath formed steam as they jogged off over the recreation ground and up the track.

"That's a full moon, Jay."

"Almost."

The great silver circle, veined in blue, was surrounded by a frosty halo. It bathed the downs in an eerie, pale light. The woods lay deep and dark in the great dip in the hills. Lookout Rock loomed above them like – like a gigantic skull, thought Jay, and shivered. It was one thing talking about an adventure like this in some cosy flat in the village, it was quite another to be out in the wide, weird world. He looked up at the great sweep of the night sky. He suddenly felt small and powerless. What was he up to? Risking his sanity, and all for this crazy girl...

As they eased to a fast walk, Cass looked up at the sky as well. Yes, she remembered nights like this from long ago. Wasn't that group of stars the Great Bear? She was slipping back, back to her other life long ago. The Lady-beneath-the-Lake took control of her spirit tonight, and her head filled with visions of the stars, reflected on black water.

The contractors' site on Horton's Field was now on their left. The huge machines lay still. A single light showed from the security guards' hut and there was the distant sound of dogs barking. The two young people took to the ditch, bending low. They had made it! The track lay ahead like a white scar. Jay thought he could see a flicker of light from the edge of the woods. It must be the tree house people. They never give up, do they, he thought. He had to admire them.

"Right, let's cut across this field," Jay whispered. They both jumped over a low electric fence and scuttled across open ground towards another bunch of abandoned bulldozers. A great dark shape lurched across their path, and they froze. But it wasn't a giant stag, just a startled cow! They laughed hysterically as it cantered heavily away.

"Sssh!" They both stopped giggling. There was someone ahead, a silent figure emerging from the darkness. A torch beam snapped on and picked out Cass. Jay was still hidden in the darkness.

"Run, Jay! Run!" she hissed. "They haven't seen you yet. Go on!"

Jay shot off like a hare, zigzagging across the field. Watch out for those cowpats! Yikes!

But Cass was nabbed. She did try to run, but

she just couldn't keep up. She was still unfit after all those weeks of being ill. A hand closed on her shoulder with a vice-like grip.

"Gotcha!"

"Mr Cunningham!" Jay's dad, in the uniform of a security guard, shone his torch in her face.

"Cass Day! What the blazes are you doing here at this time of night? Protesting again, huh? Going back to those tree people? Are you on your own? What would our Jay say if he knew you were out here, eh? And what about your mum?"

Cass was silent. All she could think about was their mission. How would Jay ever find the trench without her help? Hellfire and damnation!

Ray Cunningham marched her firmly back to the hut. And locked the door behind him.

"Girl, you're crazy. Haven't you done enough to stop this road? Haven't you half-killed yourself already?"

"Mr Cunningham, you won't call the police, will you? Please don't call the police!"

"My rule book says I have to. You're breaking the law. You just crossed over private land, after all. You trespassed. Were you going to paint slogans on the machinery or pour water into the diesel or something?"

"No, no, really. I was...I was just visiting friends, er...the protesters in the wood," she lied furiously, blushing.

Jay's dad stared at her. He let her go and sat down heavily. He reached in his bag and brought out a flask of hot tea. Silently, he offered her a cup, which she drank gratefully. For a whole five minutes he said nothing.

"Very well," he said finally. "I won't involve the police. But by heck I'm going to tell your mother. I tell you, she will not be pleased, young lady, not pleased at all."

He stomped over to the table and picked up a mobile phone.

"What's your number at home? Come on, Cass, if you don't tell me I can find out easily enough. And the other patrols will be back here in half an hour. If you're not gone by then I shall have to inform the police."

"870426"

"Thank-you!"

Cass sat in the hut, miserable and angry. Tears welled up in her eyes. She had let Jay down. Just like Kerak had let his village down so long ago. Life wasn't fair. At last a car's headlights filled the window and there was the crunch of tyres on the stone chip track to the site. It seemed to be time to face the music.

The door opened and her mother came in, her face grim and furious.

EYES OF THE SKULL

Chapter 11
Skull in the Mud

Jay paused at the edge of the field, out of breath, leaning against a bulldozer. The protesters had daubed the sides of the machine with graffiti. BUZZ OFF BZ and MO-WAY NO-WAY read the slogans.

It was a shame that Cass had been caught, but as he dived away from the dazzle he had recognised the voice as his father's, so he knew she would be in safe hands. The trouble was, only Cass knew exactly where she had fallen into the trench that day Jay had been out cold at the time, of course, and had only the vaguest notion where it was.

Funnily enough, Jay's first feelings of fear had worn off. He was buzzing now, magic. Okay, so he was a grave-robber! So the world had gone insane! But he was sure he'd pull this one off. He owed it to Cass.

A cloud floated over the moon and the night closed in around him. The downs were now a flat silhouette. The sky lightened only to the northeast, where the streets and buildings of Sheriton gave off an orange glow that could be seen from miles away.

The wood lay ahead, inky and forbidding. It seemed to him as if all the trees were listening. Jay went forward slowly, alert as a cat out hunting. Like a cat, his eyes probed the darkness, looking for the shapes of the trees. And he had the strangest feeling that he was being watched in turn. Not by security guards or by protesters. But by some other, more mysterious force. Was it some ancient god? Or was it poor Kerak's skull, lying where it had fallen thousands of years ago, and doomed to keep watch forever? An owl screeched in the distance.

Jay followed a line of barbed wire reeled out by the contractors. Some timber lay sawn and stacked, where the contractors had started to use their chain saws. There were some trenches and mounds of soil here, but these were in the wrong place. They had markers stuck against them, probably put there by the archaeologists, thought Jay. Now, this was where he had run past the policeman during the protest. And there was that bushy holly tree on the edge of the wood. It was more of a landmark now that the other trees were beginning to lose their leaves. That was where the stag – the Horned God – had knocked him to the ground. Right!

Now, when he had recovered that day, he had wandered off – up this path. Or was it up that one? He scouted around, but it was impossible to make sense of anything in the dark. However, after about ten minutes he glimpsed a campfire through the trees and heard voices and some laughter. Somebody was blowing on a penny whistle. The tune sounded like a sad one to him. So, that must be the spot where he had met the tree house people after Cass' accident. He must be getting near to the trench.

Should he go over to the protesters now and ask for their help? Some of them would be sure to know the very point where Cass had fallen. But what would he say to them? "I've come to look for a skull that belonged to my girlfriend's brother thousands of years ago?" They'd have had him taken away and locked up! Perhaps he could just say he had lost a penknife or a wristwatch there – but then why would he come looking for it on a dark night? And they would probably insist on helping him look for it.

No, he was on his own for this one. And that was how it had to be. So he carefully stalked around the edge of the tree-people's camp and struck out at an angle from the border of the wood. In the end he walked straight into the trench, falling heavily. The slit was about two metres deep, so at least he was hidden from view. He pulled out a torch from his backpack and shone it up and down the trench. It was still full of sticky, chalky mud. No skull.

Hang on, now, hadn't Cass banged her head as she fell? And there was an excavator – left overhanging the half-finished ditch. About twenty five metres away. He slithered and squelched through the mud, remembering that poem by Wilfred Owen. So this was what it had been like to fight in trenches, as they did in the First World War. No joke.

The bucket of the excavator cast a deep shadow over the trench, blocking out even the faintest starlight. Jay pulled up the sleeves of his jacket and drew a deep breath. For some reason he shut his eyes, too. He plunged his bare arms into the cold, clammy clay. His finger closed on something cold and hard. A round flint? No bigger, bigger, this was it. He pulled and with a loud sucking noise it came free.

Jay lurched backwards and at the same time opened his eyes. The moon broke through the clouds at that very moment and lit up a skull, pale as marble, dripping with muddy water. The eyes, the eyes were so empty and yet Jay could swear they were seeing everything. Jay shuddered and felt sick. Pins and needles seemed to run up and down his arms. And then he realised that his whole body was shaking – with fear? With relief?

For a moment Jay cradled the ancient skull in his hands, awkwardly but gently, like the time he had held a newborn baby at his mum's hospital. Then he took the woollen scarf from his neck and wrapped up the skull in a bundle, which he placed in his backpack.

Right, time to get away from the wood. He loped up to the gully beneath Lookout Rock and then took a long bypass around the contractors' site. This would not be the ideal time to run into his dad again!

As Jay ran, it was as if he no longer had to think where he put his feet. He just flowed, like the breeze that was now picking up and blowing through the trees. And a strange fancy entered Jay's head. It was as if he was running alongside someone. A young, red-headed warrior, on some moonlit night long ago. They were chanting a hunting song that helped them keep up a steady pace. The village lay ahead.

RUN, RUN, RUN! It was not my sister who came to my rescue, but her young friend, the black-skinned warrior. He held me so carefully in his hands. Nobody has touched or held me since the day I died. I do not know where he is taking me, but I feel that this is the beginning of the end, the end of my long vigil on the downs.

This is a kind and a good friend. And he is swift, not like that foolish old man who fell asleep by the wood. If there are more people like Jay the woods may yet be saved and the gods may rest in peace.

We run now just as I used to run with my friends on frosty moonlit nights, when the geese came flying in for winter and the owls screeched and hooted in the forest. My spirit is racing alongside the black-skinned warrior and I rejoice. My sister has chosen well. I am running home at last.

☠

When Jay reached the outskirts of the village he slowed his pace to a walk. At Cass' house he saw her mum at the front door, talking to that policeman again. He bolted down the alley and came around the back way. A light was on in Cass' bedroom. He threw some gravel at the window pane a couple of times, and then the curtain drew back.

"Jay!" she leaned out of the window. "How did you get on? Sorry, I can't come out. I've been grounded! Mum was really furious!"

Jay clambered on to the fuel tank at the rear of the house and took off his backpack. He drew out the bundle and raised it above his head in triumph. Cass stretched downwards and, just able to reach, took it from him and clutched it to her chest.

Chapter 12
Blackout!

While Jay slipped home to have a shower and get some sleep, Cass unwrapped the bundle and placed the skull on her desk. She stared at it in fascination, at first with absolute horror. She had never held a skull before. She imagined the worms that had been wriggling through its mouth, the flesh that had been pecked away.

But she pushed such thoughts from her mind. A feeling of love and affection began to grow inside her. After all, this had been poor Kerak, her one-time brother.

As she stared at the skull, Cass seemed to pass into a trance-like state. It was as if her room filled with the sweet smell of the forest, the scent of wild flowers and the smoke of campfires. The posters on the wall, her junk and jumble of clothes, all faded into a haze. She thought she could see Kerak alive again, smiling and raising his hand in greeting. She tried to talk, but then it seemed to her that Kerak put his finger to his lips and shook his head.

There was a sharp tap on the door. Cass did a rapid roll across the bed and hurriedly pulled a sweater over to cover up the skull. Her mother came in and sat on the windowsill, her arms folded.

"Cass, we must have a talk."

Cass snapped back to cold reality. "We've had one. You grounded me."

"Well, what on earth did you expect? I'm *not* having you getting mixed up in the road protests again. School starts next week and I want you to be fit and well, not dashing around the countryside in the dead of night. Do you hear me?"

"You've been talking to your policeman friend, have you?"

"Look, Cass, Phil's just a friend. I'm not discussing you with him, I assure you. And I don't yet intend to talk about him to you. I have my own life to lead. No, this one's between you and me."

"The road has to be stopped, you just don't understand."

"But I do!"

"You do *NOT*. It could mean a disaster, a real disaster! Worse than anything this village has ever seen!"

Lizzie looked at Cass severely.

"Don't you think you're exaggerating just a tiny bit? You do know that I support you, Cass. I don't want them to build that motorway link either. And it may surprise you to know that even Phil agrees with me. You shouldn't have been so rude to him. But this road business is hardly worth risking your life over, Cass, is it? Maybe you don't realise just how ill you have been."

Cass pulled a face. She was about to argue

back when all the lights suddenly flickered.

"Oh no, what was that?" cursed Lizzie Day. "What's up with the electricity?"

"There seems to be a power surge or something…"

The lights flickered again – and went out. Lizzie looked out of the window.

"I don't think it's just a fuse. All the other houses are out, it's not only us. Why do we still get power cuts, for heaven's sake? These scientists can fly us to the moon but they can't even make sure we get a regular supply of electricity. What about our freezers, fridges, computers, heating for the elderly?" The wind began to rise and the alarm began to ring in the shop below.

"Uh-oh. I'd better go and sort that out. Look, ring the electricity company for me, will you?" Lizzie found a torch and went downstairs.

The sound of the alarm had woken Will, who got up and peered sleepily around his door, into the corridor.

"What's up, sis?" Cass put the phone down. "The power's out, Will. All over the village."

"Cass, I'm a bit scared," said Will hesitantly. That was unlike him. "I was having nightmares. There were all these baddies coming to get me. Their faces were painted blue. They were waiting for me outside school."

"Hey, hey, Will. Don't worry, there's nothing wrong. Everything will be all right."

"Cass, where's Mum?"

"She's downstairs. The shop alarm went off in the wind."

"Sis... if there is a power cut, why have you got light in your room?" Will pointed.

Cass swung round. A pale shimmering glow was coming through her door.

"Get back to bed at once," she snapped to Will, and swung around, diving back into her bedroom. She pulled the door shut and locked it.

The skull, no longer covered by her sweater, was radiating light. It appeared to pulsate and was haloed in hazy blue light. Little crackles of electricity came from those sad, empty eye sockets. Shadows flickered across the wall, like wild beasts.

Cass reached out to touch the skull, but was thrown with some force back on to her bed. She felt icy cold and dizzy. And scared.

"Kerak! Kerak!" she moaned.

A deep voice echoed through her head, as if through a cave. "I answer for Kerak. I, the Horned God, the Stag of the Forest. I speak to you, you who act for the Lady-beneath-the-Waters. You and your companion have done well. But warn your friends in the modern times that we, the ancient gods, wish to continue our sleep in peace. In peace. In peace..."

The voice faded away, and with it the blue light. Cass thought she caught a glimpse of Kerak again, only this time he seemed to be sleeping and at peace. Then that vision too disappeared. She covered up the skull again and lay back on her bed, stunned.

Outside, a great blast of wind suddenly swept down Crickstone High Street, sending fallen leaves into swirls. Some old people later swore they had heard the bellow of a stag and the drumming of hooves, that night. The younger villagers poured scorn on them. They said they must have just heard plastic dustbin lids clattering down the road...

☠

Cass' mum came back indoors and shone a torch into her room.

"Cass, I've fixed the shop alarm. There's quite a wind blowing up out there. Cass? Are you all right?"

"Umm, yeah..." Cass' voice was low and hesitant. "But Will's been having nightmares. Go in and make sure he's all right."

"Did you ring the electricity company?"

"Yes, they said they were still checking it out."

But just then the lights came back on. Lizzie breathed a sigh of relief and went into Will's room. What a tip, she must get him to tidy up! She tiptoed over piles of toys and games and comics. Her youngest was fast asleep again, as if he didn't have a care in the world. She kissed him. What a night! It was time they all got some sleep.

They did, but it was certainly a restless night. Jay tossed and turned, dreaming of drowning in mud. Cass fell into a deep sleep at last, all her energies drained. Will dreamed he was fighting a dinosaur with a water pistol, while his mum dreamed of a certain policeman. And Mr Bodgett dreamed he was sending his wife to prison – for a life sentence.

The wind gusted stronger and stronger. It howled over the downs and whined around the ruined towers of Crickstone Castle. It set off car alarms. It knocked over display signs outside the garage. But funnily enough it didn't harm the tree people, as they camped on the edge of the forest. Perhaps they were sheltered from the worst of it, under the lee of Lookout Rock. Or perhaps the Horned God was protecting them.

But if so, he certainly wasn't protecting the contractors. Coming off shift at dawn, Ray Cunningham found that the wind had brought down the power lines, leaving a tangle of wreckage. And a big oak had come down right across the lane, blocking the way.

"I just don't believe it!" he said to himself, pulling down his cap and turning up his collar. "Is there a jinx on this job, or what?"

Chapter 13
Puzzle Page

Lizzie Day realised that Cass had started locking the door to her bedroom, but she didn't make a fuss. Teenagers were like that. If she wanted privacy, that was fair enough. Perhaps Cass just wanted to stop Will reading her precious diary.

If Lizzie had known that her daughter had an ancient skull in there, she would certainly not have forgiven her for that night-time expedition.

But she didn't know and so Cass was no longer grounded. Two days of being shut up in the house had driven her crazy. But now it was the weekend and she was sitting in Crickstone's old bus shelter with Jay. Not that they were going anywhere. It was just a place to get out of the cold. The gales were still blowing unusually fiercely.

Between them on the bench was the local newspaper, flapping furiously in the draught. Cass struggled to hold it flat.

M-WAY PLANS TO GO AHEAD.
Appeal rejected, protesters told.

The headlines said it all.

Jay, jammed up against the stone wall of the shelter, blew a bubble from the gum he was chewing. *Pop.*

Cass looked at him. "Jay, we've got to go back to the wood and bury Kerak's skull."

She hadn't told her friend about the light and the voices during the power cut. She was afraid he would finally flip. But perhaps Jay had changed since finding the skull. He no longer seemed to doubt that the past and the present were tied together in some way. Since he had felt Kerak's spirit running by his side – and he hadn't told Cass about that – it was as if he had joined Cass on this crazy roller coaster between two worlds.

"You're right," said Jay. "So what do we have to do? Can you remember anything about this burial place from your past life?"

"No," replied Cass. "I have tried and tried, but I remember nothing. I think Kerak told me that only boys and men were taught where the sacred place of the Horned God was to be found. I'm sure the women and girls had their own secret places. When I was travelling back in time I saw a vision of blue-heads swarming all over the forest, and the women from our village were secretly taking the bodies of our fallen warriors to some deep shaft on the hillside. I may even have been one of those women. But the downs have changed so much over the ages..."

Cass folded up the flapping newspaper and shook her head from side to side, as if to get rid of all those dreamy ideas. Then she rummaged in the plastic bag beside her on the bench and brought out her diary. It was crammed with postcards and addresses and doodles. But at the end of the diary there was still some space, and there she had jotted down all she could remember of her dream-like conversation with Kerak.

"His first words were 'the Horned God appears amongst us in times of trouble as a leaping stag with burning eyes'. Okay, that's already happened. You saw the stag, and so did the old tramp." Cass paused. "We have to bury Kerak's skull in the secret dwelling place of the Horned God. It was the holy place of his – of my – clan. 'Our brave warriors sleep in his dark halls until the end of time.'"

"So how do we find it?"

"Kerak gave me some clues. They were a bit like riddles, which he had learned by heart from the holy man of our tribe. It is somewhere that is high, but low. Now I think that must mean that it is high in the downs, but deep down in the earth. Perhaps in some cave or pothole."

"Well, people do still go potholing up there," broke in Jay. "We did that lesson at school, on how rainwater soaks through the chalk and carves out caves and tunnels underground. And do you remember the archaeologist at the appeal? She said that the Stone Age miners carved out pits and chambers to get at the flints in the chalk. I reckon the downs must be a honeycomb of underground passages."

"Right!" Cass' eyes lit up excitedly. "The place we are looking for is wet but dry according to Kerak," she went on. "I suppose that could mean that it is surrounded by a pool or a spring, but perhaps on an island or a dry rock. But the next bit is tough. It says 'amongst the oak roots but amongst the clouds'."

Jay blew another bubble. "You've got me there. Oak roots, okay, so it is underground. But clouds? They could be reflected in the pool I suppose. *But* this is meant to be in the depths of the earth. Pass!"

"There were other directions, too. 'To approach his dwelling you must become a fish, a mole, a spider, a fly.' Any ideas?"

Jay chewed his gum and thought. "Fish swim, moles go underground. Spiders? I just don't know."

"Spiders spin webs. Maybe we'll need a net. Or rope," Cass continued excitedly. "And flies?"

"Eat disgusting things!" chipped in Jay, just like his old self.

"Ha, ha!" Cass punched him on the shoulder. "Flies – fly? How can we fly underground? Buzz? Crawl on the ceiling?"

Jay shrugged. "Did Kerak tell you anything else?" he asked. Cass frowned. "He taught me some verses. Well, they were like spells, really. Heaven knows what they meant. I doubt he even knew. But he said they had to be recited at the 'end of time'."

"Look, I'm freezing," said Jay suddenly.

"Let's go and talk about this somewhere cosier!"

They huddled inside their jackets. Cass stole Jay's baseball cap and pulled it down over her eyes.

"Give it back, Miss Flintstone!"

Cass stuck her tongue out at him. They set off down the street. Black clouds were scudding across a yellow sky. Crossing the road, Cass fumbled for her keys. She was about to open the door to her house, when it flew open. Out hurtled a hideous skull with a grinning mouth. Below it was a white sheet, like a shroud.

Cass screamed loud and long, until it seemed that every window in the street would shatter. Her mum came running out of the shop. A cyclist ran up on the pavement and crashed into a litter bin. Jay grabbed at the sheet – and revealed Will.

Will pushed his skull mask up over his forehead.

"Hallowe'en!" he chuckled crazily. "You'd forgotten, it's Hallowe'en tonight. I fooled you! Trick or treat! The spooks are out on the prowl!"

Lizzie joined in the general laughter. But Cassie was white and shaking.

"Will," she gasped. "You shouldn't – scare people like that. It's not fair." She and Jay stamped into the house and slammed the door.

"That's the trouble with my big sister," grumbled Will to his mum. "She can't take a joke any more."

"Oh, let her be," sighed Lizzie Day, going

back into the shop. When would her children ever learn to behave sensibly, like other people's kids?

Indoors, Cass went to check that her room was still securely locked. It was, the skull was safe.

"There was one other thing, Cass," said Jay, now sitting on the arm of the sofa. "You said you thought that the spiral maze we saw in that library book was the same as the pattern of Kerak's tattoo. And that it might hold the key. What did you mean exactly?"

Cass pulled yet another page out of her diary.

"I copied it down, look." She spread the sheet of paper out on the sofa. "Don't you think it might be a map? Of how to reach the sacred site? The pattern was obviously a very important one to the tribe. It must have had some great religious meaning to them."

"Good thinking. I wonder if it could be a map of the tunnels and caves deep inside the downs? Where exactly did the book say it was?"

"That's the trouble," said Cass. "It didn't. Can you believe it, the book just doesn't say where it was drawn."

"And the book was printed back in the 1930's. By now that carving could be completely covered with moss or ivy."

Cass and Jay went into the kitchen and so they didn't hear the front door open. They looked round to see Will, still in his Hallowe'en costume, holding up the picture of the maze.

"Give that here at once, idiot," exploded

Cass in renewed fury. "Haven't you caused enough trouble for one day?"

"What's the big deal, sis?" Will laughed. "What do you want this silly old picture for anyway?"

"I'm not telling you," snapped Cass. "You wouldn't understand."

"Oh, wouldn't I?" smirked Will. At times like this he could drive Cass into a rage. "As it happens, I do understand."

"Hold on," broke in Jay. "Just what exactly do you understand?"

"This picture," said Will proudly, "is on a stone up in Crickstone Wood."

"You've seen it?" exclaimed Cass.

"With my own eyes. I went up there once with Connor. Last year. It was a really spooky place. I was scared." Suddenly, Will seemed rather timid and babyish. Cass put her arm round him.

"Will, this is really important. I can't tell you why. But could you tell me exactly where the carving is?"

"I suppose I could," said Will. "What's it worth?"

"As much chocolate as you can eat without being sick," said Cass.

"You're on!" replied Will, grinning his annoying grin once more.

Cass decided. School started again on Tuesday. On Monday morning they would take the skull to its proper resting place.

Chapter 14
Storm Sunday

Now the appeal against the motorway link had been turned down, new protesters were pouring into Crickstone from all over the country, even from abroad. There were television crews in the High Street and Mrs Bodgett was interviewed on the national news. Mr Bodgett took their television set to the local rubbish dump in a rage.

The protesters' camps now spread along the borders of the whole wood, decorated with colourful flags and banners. The contractors had increased their security patrols, and Ray Cunningham certainly had his hands full.

The tree fellers were ordered to start work again on Monday morning. This time the company was determined to get rid of the protesters once and for all and to move in the heavy earth moving machinery without further delay. They had lost enough money during the delays caused by the appeal.

The Sheriton police too were making sure that the events of the summer would not be repeated. The law was on the side of the contractors, and that was all there was to it. P.C. Phil Sergeant could see the sense of that, and would do his duty. But he did want the whole affair sorted out peacefully. And he wasn't too sure that the plans put forward by Sergeant

Hanway were the best way of avoiding trouble.

On the Sunday afternoon, police from all over the county were moved into the Crickstone area. Phil Sergeant was none too happy to lose his weekend break. Or to have Hanway in his patrol car. As he drove over to the village, he passed vans and rain-soaked hitchhikers all heading for the protest camps. He hoped Lizzie Day's daughter was keeping out of mischief this time.

The weather was appalling. Rain hammered on the car windows and on the roof. Why did the road protests always seem to bring out the worst in the weather? It seemed to be dark already and it was only two in the afternoon. The patrol car drove up behind a huge truck, which was slowly taking a bulldozer to the road site. Its tyres spat up a wall of muddy water which sprayed their windscreen. Phil Sergeant overtook and cautiously took the long curve before the turn off to Crickstone.

The road here passed through ploughed fields, waterlogged and gloomy in the autumn storm. Dense thickets of blackthorn and bramble covered the verges. Phil Sergeant suddenly swerved as a great, dark shape leaped across the road in front of the car. The tyres skidded on the wet road and the car slewed round.

"What the – !" Hanway cursed.

The patrol car lights picked out a shaggy mud-coated hide, huge branching antlers and eyes that seemed to glow with the fires of hell.

The animal plunged with a crash into the undergrowth on the right-hand verge and disappeared into the sheets of rain.

"A giant deer? Am I seeing things?" Hanway looked at Phil Sergeant. The policeman was trying to restart the car, which had stalled. But it wouldn't fire. The engine turned and turned and then died away with a sick moan. The lights went out. The radio was dead.

"This car was only serviced last week!" Hanway thumped the dashboard with his fist. "But one bit of damp and it's a goner! Blasted deer!"

The big lorry was now looming down the curve behind them. Hanway leaped out of the car and waved down the driver. There was a great swooshing of air brakes as the lorry slowed.

Phil Sergeant pushed the patrol car into a safe position by the side of the road. He wasn't worried about the car. He was worried about something else. The words of Jacko, the old tramp, rang through his head. "It was twice the size of any real deer, with eyes that burned right through me." The 'Horned God', Jacko had called it. Phil began to doubt his own judgment. But both he and Hanway had seen something unearthly, he was sure of that.

The truck driver radioed in to base, but it was an hour before a replacement car arrived and the broken-down vehicle was towed back to Sheriton. A bad start. And when they eventually reached Crickstone, things got worse.

The power was off again and the whole village was in darkness. The River Crick had burst its banks and flooded over the recreation ground. Black, muddy waters had begun to lap at the High Street itself. Lizzy Day was busy in the shop, trying to seal off the front door with rolled sheets. Sandbags would do the trick, but they had all been taken by surprise. Will was meant to be helping her, but mostly he was tearing across the street to splash around in his wellies.

Above the shop, Cass was sitting in her bedroom, with the door firmly locked. The curtains were drawn tightly, but she could hear the raindrops drumming on her window. Cass had lit two candles by Kerak's skull. The room was filled with a flickering light. The candles were more than a source of light, they burned in honour of Kerak and his memory. It was more like a candlelight vigil in some old church.

Cass stared at the skull and it still seemed to glow with a faint blue light, radiating a weird energy.

"Tomorrow, Kerak, tomorrow. Your long wait is nearly over." Dreamily, she seemed to see him again, his long hair blowing in the wind on Lookout Rock.

She thought she heard his voice again, too. "The Lady of the Waters-Beneath-the Earth is becoming restless too. The waters are rising, rising. She is calling to you to do your duty..."

☠

Jay hadn't realised how bad the storm was until he decided to go and see Cass, to make the final plans for tomorrow's expedition. He was soaked to the skin in two seconds flat. His jeans were plastered to his legs.

No sooner was he on the street than all the lights went out in the village. "Uh-huh Kerak," he muttered to himself. "Up to your old tricks again? Which gods are you inviting into town tonight?"

He had his answer sooner than he expected, stepping into a full metre of cold, black swirling water at the end of a back alley. "Ugh! So it's that old Lady of the Lake, I guess!" Now his feet were squelching as he backtracked to higher ground.

Turning in by the village clock, Jay saw an angry crowd. And never learning from past experience, he walked over to see what the trouble was. Beams of torches lit up faces and figures in the darkness, but it was hard to make out what was going on.

A group of police officers was standing opposite a group of road protesters. Feral Tribe members by the look of them, from the woods. Jay noticed that Phil Sergeant was one of the policemen, but they were being led by a sergeant he hadn't seen before, a man with a heavy black moustache and an angry red face.

"Out!" Hanway was shouting. "I want you

out of this village at once!"

"What's his problem?" Jay asked one of the protesters, a pale-faced bloke about three or four years older than him.

"He says we've left our van blocking the road into the village. The fact is it just packed up. Must be the rain. It's hardly our fault."

Hanway was fed up. These protesters were complaining about roads, were they? So how come they owned cars and vans at all? And why didn't they look after them? He seemed to have forgotten that his own patrol car was in a similar state that afternoon. He pushed angrily at the leader of the protesters – who pushed him back.

Soon there was a rumpus going on. Jay stepped forward to hold back a hothead amongst the protesters. Hanway swung round.

"And you're nicked," he said to Jay.

Phil Sergeant raised his eyes to the heavens.

Chapter 15
Jay Arrested

Sunday night. The van drove into the yard of Sheriton police station, radio crackling. They were herded out and through the doors – three of the road protesters and Jay.

"Look, there's been some mistake. I was just trying to stop a fight," spluttered Jay to the desk officer.

"Of course you were, sonny," came the sarcastic reply. "Name? Age?" The questions came rapidly.

Jay was angry. "Look, how long is this going to take?"

"That will depend on you," said the man in blue.

But it didn't seem to depend on Jay, but on how busy the police were. And they were busy. Reports were coming in from all over the county of flooding and storm damage. Jay waited for hours but everyone seemed to ignore him. Supposing they held him all night?

He had to get word to Cass. Tomorrow was the big day – the day when they would take the skull to its final resting place, the day the contractors started work. Even if the cops let him out tonight, they would tell his parents and then he really would be in deep trouble. Even though he was totally innocent, he couldn't see his dad waiting for any explanations. Maybe his mum would understand…

At last a policewoman led Jay down the corridor into a brightly lit room. It was statement time. Sitting at the desk was P.C. Phil Sergeant.

"Oh. It's you," said Jay, immediately recognising the policeman.

"Afraid so," replied Phil Sergeant. "Now, I want to hear your version of what happened this evening. Remember, I was there myself."

For the next half hour, Jay described the events of the evening. No, he had not been involved in the road protests. Yes, he had been there at the first protest when he had run past the policeman. Yes, he had been at the appeal in Sheriton. But he was there because he was interested, not because he was a protester as such. The road had brought work for his dad, after all. Yes, he was a friend of Cass, everybody knew that. And she was well known for her part in the protest.

In the end, a cup of tea arrived for Jay. P.C. Sergeant left the room to talk to Hanway.

"Do him. For obstructing a police officer in the course of his duty!" Hanway had little time for the likes of Jay.

"Sarge, this boy has never been in trouble before," pleaded Phil. "I've heard good reports about him in the village. He's no troublemaker. I genuinely believe he meant no harm. He was actually trying to stop that protester from thumping you!"

Hanway snorted.

"You're too soft! That's always been the trouble with you."

"Well, you won't have to put up with me for much longer," retorted Phil. "As you know, I'm retiring in the new year. Now, let me give the boy a caution. I'll have a word with the parents."

"Oh, let him go then. We've got more important business in hand right now. Tomorrow's protest could turn ugly. But I want firmer action from now on. Understood?"

"Yes, Sarge," said Phil wearily.

He walked back into the interview room and sat down heavily opposite Jay. He started giving the lad a good talking to, explaining what was meant by a caution.

Just then the lights in the police station seemed to fade. They flickered back on again and then shut off.

Jay had to grin as chaos broke out in the corridor.

"Get the emergency generator going!" Hanway was screaming.

"The computer's gone down!" another voice was saying.

"Welcome to Sheriton, Kerak!" chuckled Jay.

"What did you say?"

"It seems to me that my friend Kerak has asked the Horned God to visit you!" laughed Jay recklessly.

In the darkness, P.C. Sergeant sat up with surprise. There was that phrase again. The 'Horned God'. The phrase that Jacko had used in this very room. The policeman understood less and less. But now was not the time for questions. He had to leave the room to sort out the chaos.

"Stay right where you are, Jay. If you try to do a runner now, we'll come down on you like a ton of bricks."

After a full five minutes the lights clicked back on and the computers started up again. But Phil Sergeant blinked in disbelief as he caught sight of the screen over the operator's shoulder. It glowed with a blue light and in the centre was – a skull. Its pale electronic bones revolved slowly, showing in X-ray the brain cavity, the teeth and finally two huge, empty eye-sockets.

"What on earth is that?" exclaimed Phil.

"Some silly idiot must be playing tricks on us," said the operator, hitting the quit key. "Some prankster from police headquarters. Last night was Hallowe'en, after all."

The skull image lingered and then gradually faded. Up came the more familiar menu on the screen. Phil Sergeant laughed with relief.

When he returned to the interview room, Jay was sprawled across the chair, half asleep. Phil shook him by the shoulder.

"Jay, just as we were so rudely interrupted, you began to tell me about some friend of yours. Kerak was it? Is he one of the protesters? Are you mixed up in something you can't handle?"

Jay eyed him.

"No."

"No what?"

"No, he isn't one of the protesters. And no, I'm not mixed up with some sinister plot."

"Who or what is the Horned God? Is it some code word?" Phil Sergeant wanted to get to the bottom of all this.

"Horned God? I've no idea." Jay was suddenly wary. He mustn't put Cass' mission in danger, by giving away too much.

The policeman continued, like a dog worrying at a bone.

"You used the phrase 'Horned God', I heard you. Just as the power failed. Now I've heard that phrase before. I've seen some strange things today. I want you to explain."

"There's nothing to tell you." Jay searched wildly for an answer. "The Horned God thing, that's just a line from a film. *Hallowe'en Horror*. We got it out on video last week."

Phil Sergeant knew that Jay was lying. Something was going on here. But it was clear he wasn't going to get anywhere tonight.

"Can I go home now?" asked Jay.

Phil thought for a moment.

"Sorry Jay, I want you to stay in overnight. There's a few more questions I want to ask you tomorrow morning. If I get the answers I want, you will be free to go."

Jay shook his head. "I have to go now. You don't understand. It's really important. I'm busy tomorrow."

"Doing what?"

"That's none of your business."

"Then I'm afraid you have to stay here, Jay.
Look, it really is late now. It's best for you to
stay here anyway. There are no more buses into
Crickstone at this time of night. And I'm not
going to drive you home. Your dad will be out
at work, right? So look, just stay here. It's no
big deal."

Jay sighed. He appealed to the policeman's
good nature.

"Look, can you get a message to Cass Day?
You're big pals with her mum these days, right?
Don't tell her I was arrested or anything. Just
tell Cass: 'Solo!'"

"Okay, okay." Phil Sergeant wanted to know
what the message meant. But he could always
find out in the morning. Maybe these kids were
all just playing games with him, like that time
the Crickstone gang had stolen his car. And yes,
he would give Lizzie Day a call when he went off
shift. He needed a good talk with someone.

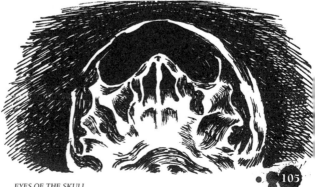

Chapter 16
Cass goes Solo

Before she went down to the shop to do the Monday morning papers, Lizzie left a hand-written note for Cass on the breakfast table. Cass was puzzling over it now. "Phil rang last night. He passed on a message for you from Jay - SO LOW."

Why had Jay been talking to that policeman? Why wasn't he here as arranged? And what did he mean? Was he trying to tell her that the burial place wasn't up on the downs as they had imagined? What had he discovered? Or was he just feeling depressed, in low spirits...?

"So low, so low, so low..." Cass read it aloud to herself. "Solo? Solo!" Perhaps her mum had misheard the message over the phone. Solo! She had to go it alone. What had happened to Jay? She felt sure he wouldn't have let her down if he had any choice in the matter. But she really had to go for it today. This was the last chance. Tomorrow was the end of the half-term holiday. The wood would be felled today if the protesters couldn't stop it. And the ancient gods were becoming angry. She had no doubt that the wild weather and the floods were a warning. This was the last chance to carry out a job that had been waiting to be done for thousands of years.

A feeling of fear swept through her whole body. How could she carry out such an enormous task all on her own? Why was it up to her of all people, Cass Day, to be serving gods that everyone had forgotten about long ago? And then she remembered that magical day when she met Kerak in her dream. She couldn't fail her brother now. She had a duty to carry out. And she wouldn't really be alone. Kerak's spirit would be beside her.

Right. She filled a small backpack. A torch, one of those ones you strap around the head. Tough nylon rope she had bought in Sheriton. A large-scale Ordnance Survey map of Crickstone Wood. Her copy of the maze pattern. Some chocolate biscuits in case she got hungry.

She now put on a sweater and a waterproof jacket. One last thing. The skull of Kerak. She made sure that Will was still asleep and then took the skull from its hiding place in her bedroom. She kissed it tenderly, wrapped it in a scarf and placed it in her pack.

One last look behind her, down the stairs and on to the pavement.

"Cass! What are you doing up so early!" Oh dear. Her mum was putting newspaper placards out on to the street and had seen her.

"Just going for a walk, Mum. The weather's cleared, see..."

It was true, the day was cold but the sky was now clear, a pale, washed out blue. It was a beautiful morning.

Lizzie walked over and put her hand on Cass' shoulder.

"Not lying in for once? It looks to me like you're going up to the downs."

"So? What if I am?" Cass gave her mum that rebellious look.

"Because there just happens to be the biggest road protest yet taking place in the woods today. And as you know I have absolutely forbidden you from taking part in any more protests. From now on I want you healthy, fit and concentrating on your school work."

"Mum. I'm not going to the protest."

"You promise?"

"I promise."

Lizzie looked like she still needed convincing. But her darling daughter had already set off down the street with a jaunty wave of her hand.

Cass wasn't going to make the same mistake as on her last expedition with Jay. She decided *not* to cross through Horton's Field or the construction sites, where she would risk being stopped by the security guards or questioned by the police. She walked the long way round, even though it was a hike of eight kilometres or so. Her route took her high up the downs on the opposite side of the woods. A rabbit ran across her path, white tail bobbing, startled by this early morning intruder.

Stopping after an hour and a half, Cass

could see far below. Along the bottom edge of the wood the protesters were already up and about, forming lines. She could see small vans with flashing orange lights bringing construction workers and tree fellers to the wood. Hidden down the lane she could see a whole cluster of parked blue police vans. They were clearly expecting trouble.

As she gazed at the antlike figures below, she became aware of Kerak's skull in her backpack. She felt wobbly and faint. Maybe she should have had some breakfast before leaving. She took out a chocolate biscuit and nibbled on it.

Suddenly, it seemed as if she was looking at the scene below through Kerak's eyes, through the eyes of the skull. It was a battle scene, that final dreadful battle again. The warriors of the tribe were swarming out of the village, grabbing weapons in confusion. Their blue-painted enemies had them surrounded, yelling and whooping. It was a moment of sheer terror.

And then the dream-like flash faded and Cass focused again on the crisp autumn morning, on the low sun flashing over pools of flood water on the lowland fields.

Cass shivered and pulled out the map to check her position. Yes, there should be a little path to the left about a hundred metres ahead. She folded the map and turned over the lip of the downs, plunging immediately into the darkness of the woods.

The leaves that still clung to the gnarled oak trees and the tall, smooth-barked beeches were coloured in beautiful reds and browns, but many branches were already bare of leaves, stripped by the unholy storms of the last week. One or two giant trees had been uprooted by the storms, their great roots ripped from the chalky soil.

The path rose and fell. In places it was overgrown by dense bushes and shrubs. Cass tripped over a dead branch at one point, scratching her hand on brambles. Few walkers entered the woods this way. A harsh sound tore through the morning: skraaaak! There was a flash of pinkish-brown feathers – it was a jay, wasn't it? Harmless enough. In the old days there would have been wild boar, wolves, dangerous wild animals.

After about fifteen minutes Cass came to a hollow in the wild landscape. Here the trees were spindly rowans with bright orange berries, rooted amongst rugged limestone crags. It was near here that her path joined a long track that snaked down from Lookout Rock. And it was here that Will and his little friend Connor had wandered.

Cass hoped that her brother hadn't been making up silly stories about those carved spirals. She climbed on to a ledge and searched the rock face with a keen eye. No sign. She edged sideways and realised that the rock turned inwards into a cleft. Ferns brushed her cheek. And there right in front of her eyes were the swirling lines that she had copied down so carefully. The carvings were worn and mossy. She took the sheet of paper from her pack and compared the two. An exact match. This, then, was the route to the sacred place of the Horned God, the secret burial place of the tribe. Or so she hoped.

Beside the carving was a deep, dark slit that stank of damp earth and foxes. Cass pulled out her torch and strapped it around her head. She took out the length of rope and coiled it around her waist. Drawing a deep breath, she squeezed through.

☠

Jay was finally released at about ten o'clock that morning and he went straight to Sheriton bus station. He was angry about the way he had been treated. If he had been some rich white kid, would he have been held overnight? Would he even have been arrested in the first place? P.C. Sergeant was better than that Hanway, it was true, but even he had been pestering him with all sorts of daft questions. Anyway, Jay hadn't given anything away, he was sure of that.

What now? A hard time from his dad, that was certain. Cass would be on her way by now, provided she had been given his message. He hoped she wasn't still waiting for him in the village. He couldn't go to the protest site, that was for sure. With a caution on his head and with Hanway out to get him, he would find himself back in the police station in no time.

The Crickstone bus came in and Jay jumped on board. As the bus rumbled on, Jay began to think about what Cass would be going through, trying to find that cave. He hoped she would be all right on her own and wished he could be with her. At least the weather had cleared. It was a lovely morning. But flood water still lay on the fields.

It was then that Jay had a worrying thought. The worry niggled at his brain and it grew and grew. If all the rain water had seeped down into the chalk of the downs, then the levels of water and underground springs would now be rising. Why hadn't they thought of that? Cass was in mortal danger of being cut off by the water and trapped underground!

EYES OF THE SKULL

Chapter 17
Bats and Spiders

Cass found herself in a dank, dark, musty cave. Water dripped from the ceiling of the cave, plop, plop, plop. Her head-torch arched wildly around the chamber. There were spikes of dripping limestone coming down from the ceiling. Stalactites, were they called? Or stalagmites? She should have done her homework.

The torch beam then swung around to light up – what? Cass automatically ducked in horror. The ceiling was covered in ugly living things, all leathery wings and little claws. Bats! Hanging in clusters, squeaking horribly. Disturbed, one bat with a hideous snout swooped down towards her. She screamed! Just imagine it flapping, tangled in her long hair! She stopped to tie back her hair, remembering all those vampire films where Dracula turned into a bat by night... Luckily, this little demon veered away into the darkness.

Cass gulped. Some welcome! Her torch now revealed a path leading sharply downwards. "High but low," Kerak had said. Well, this was it. She followed a narrow passageway which curved to the right as it descended.

There were ancient carvings on the wall. No wonder. Long after humans had stopped living in caves, people had used them as shelter from the weather, as a place to hide from enemies, as a place to store supplies. She knew that one cave in these woods had been used as an ammunition dump during the Second World War. Her granddad had told her that, when she was little.

After five minutes, the underground passage forked. Cass held up her copy of the carving. Yes, it made sense! The circle at the centre had to be the burial ground. These lines were the passageways. At the next fork she took a left and then a right, following the plan.

As she went down into the depths of the earth, the ceiling of the rock passage became lower and lower. She was forced to hunch herself up and, in the end, crawl. So this was what Kerak had meant by "being a mole"! She felt a growing sense of being shut in, of the earth closing in around her, of being buried alive.

She inched forward, scraping her body against the rock. Her face brushed into old cobwebs and she yelped as a spider with hairy legs scuttled away over her face and neck. Spiders, deep underground? Good grief!

Suddenly, to her relief, the passage widened out again and she could stretch out a bit. Soon she could stand again. Just. But her troubles were far from over. Ahead, the passage dropped into darkness. She tossed a pebble over. Ping! It bounced away into nothingness. Too far to jump.

Time to "be a spider". She uncoiled the rope

114

and tied it round a pinnacle of rock. Closing her eyes and praying, she let the rope take the strain. It was firm. She climbed down the rope gingerly, pushing herself away from the rock face with her feet. She soon hit the ground.

But this was not dry ground. The bottom of the next passage was now filling with water. It was bubbling up through pebbles and trickling down the rock walls, black and icy cold. Soon it was up to Cass' waist. Her legs ached as she waded onwards. The water reached her chest. It was time to "be a fish".

Cass was a strong swimmer, but this performance would hardly have won her a master's badge at Sheriton Swimming Pool. Weighed down by wet clothing, weary, she struck out. She made sure that the torch stayed dry, keeping her head above the water. Her pack with its precious contents was wet through, but still safely fastened.

After what seemed like an eternity, Cass thought she could see a glint of light ahead of her. Soon she could see two ledges running along both sides of the passage. She hauled herself out of the water and straddled the gap, one foot on each ledge. Her arms were braced against the rock walls. She felt she was crawling over the ceiling and remembered the words of Kerak: "Be a fly".

At the end of the passage, the water drained away into a chalky pool. Cass collapsed onto a dry patch of rock and rolled over, exhausted.

Her head torch lit up a series of shapes across the passage ceiling. She slowly focused. They were paintings rising like beautiful butterflies across the rock. Pictures of wild animals, more like the ones seen in zoos than the ones seen around Crickstone today. Bison, wild goats – and a gigantic stag with branching antlers.

Cass rolled to the left. There was the painted figure of a bearded man dressed in skins, dancing. He wore antlers on his head. Around him were the marks of many hands, stencilled on to the rock wall. Cass knew by instinct that these paintings were very, very old. They were older by far than Crickstone village, they were already ancient when she and Kerak roamed the hills. They were pictures of the Horned God.

Cass crawled forward slowly and drew back with a gasp. She was poised on the edge of a sheer cliff. Far below her were – clouds – and roots. She remembered Jay's upside-down view of the earth and sky! And then she realised that she was looking into a reflection, in deep black water. Looking upwards, she saw that a tiny shaft led upwards. A hundred metres above her this narrow chimney opened through a tangle of roots to the bright, bright sky. Up there in the real world, the sun was shining on the downs and clouds were sailing by.

Now Cass looked forward. Ahead of her she could just make out a vast cave, a cathedral carved from rock stained with bat droppings.

She could hear the little creatures squeaking again, somewhere in the gloom. She felt more friendly towards them by now. At least there were other living creatures down here with her in the depths of the earth.

Cass now took off her pack. Water streamed from it in rivulets. She sat down with her back against the rock wall and fumbled with the fastenings.

Kerak's skull was safe. Cass breathed a sigh of relief as she unwrapped her soaking scarf. The white dome of ancient bone was glowing again, as it had done in her bedroom back home. It was soon surrounded by a halo of blue light which became brighter and brighter until it filled the whole great cave.

Cass could now see that the ledge on which she was sitting curved around the chamber. And in the centre of the underground lake there rose a flat-topped tower of rock. "Wet but dry", that's right. Her copy of the maze had been lost in the long swim, but she had no doubt. This great cave was the sacred place of the gods, the final resting place for the warriors of her clan.

Staggering to her feet, Cass raised the glowing skull to her lips.

"Goodbye, dearest Kerak!" she whispered. "Sleep well." She weighed the skull in one hand. Up came her arm and she hurled the skull through the air, across the water. A great arc of light cut through the darkness.

Suddenly the daylight from the narrow shaft dimmed, as did the torch on Cass' head. On the central tower of rock a great stag with flashing red eyes rose up, ringed in a rainbow light. It let out a loud bellow which echoed and echoed through the caves. And then the stag bounded into the air and vanished.

There was a moment's silence and then Cass heard a distant singing. And the dull thud of a skin drum. This was a tune she hadn't heard for thousands of years. The marching song of the forest tribe. Bathed in orange and blue light, she saw the ghostly forms of her people gathering in every passageway of the rocks, rising from the waters, scrambling over the rocks. The song grew stronger and stronger till the whole great cave boomed with sound. The warriors of her clan were on the march again, summoned by the bellowing of the Horned God. And this time Kerak was marching with them. To defend the woods for the very last time.

As the warriors marched by her, she was sure that one of them bent down and touched her on the cheek.

"Thank you, my brave sister," whispered the ghost. "Thank you."

I HAVE COME HOME. MY SISTER CASS HAS RISKED HER LIFE FOR ME. SHE HAS TAKEN ME BACK TO THE SACRED CAVE. I have rejoined my friends, my family, my band of warriors.

Ever since I failed to keep watch on that fateful day, I have had to watch over the forest, seeing it destroyed, year by year. That was my duty. Now at last I have been able to bring warning of the final battle for the trees. I have passed word to the dead chieftains and holy men of my people.

Now I have been forgiven. I carry the banner of the Horned God himself. We march against the destroyers of the forest.

Chapter 18
Trapped Underground

The song died away and the cave became dark. Once again the only light came from the narrow chimney leading to the top of the downs. And from Cass' pathetic little torch.

Cass stared upwards longingly. If only she could just fly upwards, like a bird or a bat. But there was no way she could climb up there. The sides of this natural chimney were crumbling and dangerous. It was impossible.

There was only one way out – the way she had come. The thought of struggling back filled her with weariness.

"Perhaps I shall die here," she said to herself. "Perhaps my skull will lie here in this holy place forever. Perhaps I was buried here anyway, thousands of years ago. My old self. Is it possible to meet oneself face to face?"

She tried to imagine what her own skull would look like.

But then Cass thought of her mum and Will – and Jay... and pulled herself together. Come on girl. Let's get back to normality. Whatever that is! She didn't need her little backpack any more, so she left it on the ledge. She didn't notice that a little mirror she owned slipped out of one of its pockets.

Cass now crawled back like a fly over the gully. She waded and swam. Her head was bruised and her hands were grazed. Soon she splashed into trouble. Deep trouble. Her foot became trapped in a rocky crevice. However much she wriggled and struggled she could not break free. Soon she had no strength left.

It was then that she realised that the waters were rising. Minute by minute. She felt them creeping up over her body, over her neck. She strained and strained, salty tears of desperation flowing into the swirling torrent.

Cass was on the verge of blacking out, when she suddenly broke into an ancient chant. Without thinking. It came from deep inside her. Another song that hadn't been heard on the downs for many a long year. It was the hymn sung by the priestesses of her tribe to the Lady of the Waters-beneath-the-Earth.

"Otter-woman, newt-woman, eel-woman, silver salmon, reflection of the stars, save us, serve us in our hour of need…"

☠

"She did WHAT?"

Phil Sergeant thumped the roof of the patrol car in fury. Just when he was due to join the operation against the road-protesters, young Jay Cunningham had come racing up the lane demanding to see him. With the worst possible news about Cass Day.

"She's gone into the cave system under the wood. To bury the skull."

"What skull, for heaven's sake?" The policeman had yet another flashback to old Jacko's drunken warning.

"There's no time to explain," stuttered Jay. "We must get Cass out. The waters will be rising, won't they, as all that rainwater sinks down through the chalk."

"Has she ever been potholing or caving?" asked the policeman. "Is she properly equipped? Has she got a helmet and so forth?"

"No," admitted Jay. "She did go on a climbing course once, I think. I doubt she had a helmet..."

"Oh you kids are so *stupid*," shouted Phil Sergeant, genuinely angry. "What shall I tell her mum when her body's carried out? Why should good people have to risk their lives saving the stupid ones?"

"Cass knew what she was doing. It had to be done. And anyway, it's hardly my fault," said Jay defensively.

"No," said Phil, suddenly tired. "No, I suppose it isn't. No, Jay, you did the right thing in telling me." He called up base on the car radio. "Oscar Tango, Oscar Tango. Young girl believed trapped in Crickstone Woods pothole system. Alert Caves Emergency Rescue Service in Sheriton." He radioed in Cass' name, address, mother's name, all the details. He arranged for a police car to pick Lizzie up. "Right Jay, where do you think this girlfriend of yours might be?"

It was an excited Will who led them at last to the carved stone. Lizzie could say nothing. Why did she have such a daughter, who would risk her life twice in just a few months? And what did these kids think they were up to? Some bizarre story of time travel and skulls and gods, according to Jay. They were all stark, staring mad! Where had she gone wrong?

Helicopters buzzed overhead. The cave rescue team, all geared up with rope, stretchers, helmets and lights were just entering the opening in the rocks. They had not explored this particular passage before and were taking no chances.

Jay wandered off uphill. He needed to get away from all this drama...from the protests and the rescue bid and the whole stupid world. Why hadn't he stopped Cass in her crazy fantasy? That's all it was, after all. The wild dreams of some daft girl who had been injured in the head and seen some weird visions. Okay, he had seen some of them too. Maybe they were catching. But enough was enough.

At the opening in the rocks, the first member of the cave rescue team soon came back out, shaking his head.

"The first section is easy. And there's signs that she's been this way. We found a rope tied to a rock pinnacle. But after that – well, the water is rising too high for us to carry on.

There's no point in losing two lives. I'm sorry," he added as Lizzie Day let out a wail.

Way up above them, Jay sat on a limestone crag. He saw the caver come out and he heard Cass' mum weeping. It could only mean the worst. He hit the rock until his knuckles were bleeding.

He turned away from the scene, bitterly. It was then that he noticed the black hole deep in the undergrowth. Could there be another way into the cave system? He crashed through the brambles and peered down.

Darkness, darkness. What was that pale, milky light far below. Water? But then as the sun broke out behind his head, a shaft of sunlight pierced the shaft and a dazzling flash was briefly reflected. Jay was filled with new hope.

He came charging down the forest track, yelling at the top of his voice.

"There's another way in! There's another way in!"

The rescue party raced up the track and examined the shaft which dropped sickeningly down to the main chamber. Yes, it must all be part of the same cave system. In no time at all they had rigged up ropes and tackle, and a woman was abseiling down into the darkness. Lizzie wondered how anyone could face such an ordeal. Well, Cass could, for one. Her daughter never ceased to amaze her.

The rescuer reached Cass about twenty minutes later. She heard her before she found

124

her. The sound of a haunting song in some strange language was echoing around amongst the caves and passages. Cass was standing with her mouth just above the surface of the water. By some miracle it had stopped rising just in time to save her life.

It was a long time before Cass was eventually hauled up the shaft. She was pale and shaken, but she wasn't seriously injured. Not this time. Wrapped in a blanket, she soon recovered in the sunshine and open air. She hugged her mum and Will. Lizzie was too grateful to be angry.

"Don't worry, Mum, that's it. No more adventures. It's all over now," Cass grinned.

And turning to Jay, she said, "Where were you then, partner?"

"I got pulled in by the cops!" replied Jay. Cass raised her eyebrows. "And let off," he added.

"Well, I did it, see!" Cass whispered to him proudly. "All on my own! I took Kerak home. And Jay, you tell those protesters that a whole army of ghosts is marching to join the battle. The Horned God has spoken. This will be the last battle for Crickstone Wood. Just you see!"

Chapter 19
The Final Battle

The television crew was having trouble. The reporter for lunchtime news had slipped over in the muddy field. The woman with the clipboard was trying to find him some dry clothes. The sound man was complaining that there was interference. His headphones were filled with crackling.

"It must be those police helicopters or the heavy machinery," he cursed.

"Nonsense," replied the tree hippy who was being interviewed. "The reason is that you are standing on an ancient line of magic, a magnetic force field!"

The sound man raised his eyes to the heavens. Who were these dreary, tiresome people? It was one thing to protest against a road, but quite another to drag in all this sword and sorcery tosh!

Cass was safe at home, wrapped in a cosy duvet on the sofa, drinking hot, sweet tea. Her mum had said nothing – yet. Lizzie was working in the shop. But Cass knew she would be in for a roasting before the day was through. Now Cass was watching coverage of the protest on television, while Will played in his bedroom.

Jay was watching the protest live, perched on a gate about two hundred metres from the action. And this time, keeping well out of trouble. *And* well out of the way of his dad. Presumably Ray Cunningham was still on nights. Well, Jay hoped he hadn't been drafted in to help this morning. For his dad's sake as well as for his own.

Beyond the television crew, chaos was already breaking out. A long line of protesters had linked arms. Some were shouting and yelling and waving placards. The police, in full riot gear, formed a wedge and broke through the line, holding back the heaving crowd on both sides. Now Sergeant Hanway stepped forward and impatiently waved through a convoy of vans and lorries. These were followed by the heavy machines, churning up the wet soil with their clanking tracks and giant tyres. The smell of diesel hung in the air.

Phil Sergeant was among the officers helping to hold back the crowd. What a day! Cass Day's nail-biting rescue bid, and now all this. Opposite him he saw that old Mrs Bodgett was waving her fists in the air. She was meant to be keeping the peace, so she'd better avoid the eagle eye of Sergeant Hanway. Phil had to admire her courage. From behind Phil, a young lad burst through the police lines and ran towards an excavator. He was tackled and brought to the ground. Well, better that than being crushed by heavy machinery, thought the police constable.

Now the vans opened their doors and men

in hard hats and bright green overalls swarmed up into the oak trees. There were scuffles as protesters were forced down from the branches. The ramshackle platforms they had built were soon pulled apart. Cass tightened her fists in anger as she saw several of her friends led away in handcuffs. Others scattered into the woods, chased by security guards.

Soon the chain saws were buzzing and sawdust was flying as the long blades chewed into thick, wrinkled bark and hundred year old tree trunks. High wire fences were being raised. By mid-afternoon, a large strip of the lower forest had been cleared. Branches and protesters' placards lay splintered like matchsticks, as if some giant explosion had ripped across the downs. Chug-chug-chug – dumpers bucketed to and fro. It already seemed a construction site like any other.

Cass was weeping quietly. Had she risked her life in vain? She had taken Kerak's skull to the cave, but what about the ghostly army of warriors she had seen rising from the rocks? Was it all some fevered fantasy of her mind? Had the last few months been nothing but dreams? She began to doubt herself. And then she remembered the last part of Kerak's lesson on Lookout Rock. The spells to be spoken at the end of time.

She rose to her feet, the duvet falling away in a heap on the floor. She clenched her fists, raised her head, closed her eyes, and began a slow chant:

"Spirits rise, spirits rise up, spirits rise up and fight,

The final battle is here..."

☠

Out in the field below the woods, Jay saw the protesters standing around arguing in small groups, bitter and disappointed. They seemed to have lost the battle to save the woods. Some of them even began to drift away. Jay thought about joining them. He wanted to see how Cass was, after the ordeal of the morning. If he was still allowed inside her house.

Phil Sergeant wanted to go home, too. He thought he might look in at Lizzie Day's and see how Cass was, before driving back to Sheriton. It had been a long day and it was getting late.

The autumn afternoon was certainly growing dim and chill. The low sun was turning the sky orange. A cold, damp mist was beginning to creep across the fields. It rolled towards the wood and swirled around the legs of the workers. It rose and rose, climbing higher and higher. Lights were switched on along the new fences and for a few minutes they cut through the haze, but soon they faded.

At home, Cass thumped the television set. The picture was getting worse and worse. Angrily, she fiddled with the controls.

The thud of machinery in the woods began

to fall silent and the saws spluttered to a standstill. Construction workers stopped shouting to each other and strained their ears.

"Can you hear something? A sort of drum-beat?" Sergeant Hanway asked Phil, who was patrolling the inside of the fence, picking his way through the remains of tree houses, tarpaulins and branches.

"No! Hang on... What is that?" Phil Sergeant turned his head towards the looming hillside behind him. Lookout Rock seemed to be glowing above the misty slopes and the areas of the forest that had not yet been levelled. For a moment the policeman was sure he could make out a huge, red stag with spreading antlers. Was it some trick of the setting sun? But no, the deer had a great shaggy mane around its neck and it strutted with stiff legs. It raised its great head and bellowed three times. The roar echoed down the hillside.

Phil Sergeant could now hear the swelling drumbeat that had stopped the construction workers in their tracks. And then there was a soft rustling, like the shuffle of dry autumn leaves. It grew louder and louder and then it swelled into a song. Phil couldn't understand the words, but he felt that he understood it in some way. It was menacing. It was a war song.

The floating mist was damp, cold and clinging. To the bewildered workers who now began to climb out of their diggers and excavators it seemed to smell of the earth, of damp leaves, of ancient graves. Jay turned and peered across the field. The protesters looked at each other, puzzled. They turned too, as if drawn back to the forest. The police, the security guards, all stood paralysed. They just let the protesters walk through their lines.

Jay followed them and stood next to the policeman who had been questioning him just the night before. Jay tapped Phil on the shoulder.

"It's Kerak's lot!" he whispered. "They've risen up to save the forest!"

To Phil Sergeant, the billowing mist now seemed to form into ghostly shapes, almost like human figures. By some freak of the light, the misty shapes looked like some ancient army. The spikes of broken branches could have been bristling spears and quivers of arrows.

To Jay, the warriors were real figures. As real as ghosts could be. He knew only too well what was going on.

The television reporter was saying: "The weather seems to be the winner here this evening as we bring to an end live coverage from Crickstone Wood. A heavy mist has forced the motorway builders – and the protesters – to stop for today. A further report will be included in the nine o'clock news."

Cass sat up on her sofa and peered at the scene behind the reporter's bespectacled head. In the mist she was sure she could make out figures just like those she had seen in the cave this morning. She punched the sofa in triumph.

Kerak's warriors were marching to the rescue! And wasn't that the war song she was sure she could hear them singing?

Cass cursed as the credits rolled and Will's favourite cartoon came on. She had missed the best bit.

☠

Jay wasn't sure exactly what happened next. Nor were the police. Or even the protesters, although a few of them later swore they saw an army of tattooed warriors running through the mist, climbing into trees, scrambling over sheer bramble-covered rocks where no humans could have gone.

Jay's heart seemed to stand still for a moment. The whole world seemed to stop turning. There was absolute silence. And then there was a deep growling beneath the hillside and the whole earth shook with a great roar, like the roaring of the Horned God, only a thousand times louder. Chalk slopes seemed to tremble and shift and small pebbles rained down the hillside, bouncing like bullets off the metal blades of the bulldozers.

Next there was a wrenching of tree roots and then water began to seep out of the earth, gushing forth, dribbling down, filling up old mine workings, forming little streams between the trees. The streams became rivers and the rivers became torrents. In the pools below

Crickstone Wood, where Jay often went fishing, the waters bubbled and belched as if they were full of hippos. The digging machines were soon metres deep in flood water, skewed and slewed and useless.

By nightfall the mist had cleared. The machines lay abandoned and silent. The protesters sat on top of them, the light of their lamps reflected in pools of cold, muddy water.

The Lady of the Waters-Beneath-the-Earth had not only saved Cass' life. She had also answered Kerak's call to arms.

Chapter 20
Into the Sunset

Tuesday morning was wonderful for Cass. Okay, she had to go back to school after her long break. Okay, her mum had given her the worst telling off she had heard in her life. But everything was normal again. The other world she had glimpsed seemed to be fading away for good. She was herself again, one hundred percent herself, not some Stone Age girl stuck in a loop of history.

It was great to see her mates again, although she was a bit disappointed that very few of them seemed to care about the motorway link. She had thought they would be full of the news, but most of her friends were more interested to find out whether she and Jay were still seeing each other.

Well, they were certainly seeing each other come the lunch break.

"That pizza was the nearest thing to cardboard I have ever had to eat!" exclaimed Jay, pushing back his chair.

"You should eat the salad," scolded Cass, "it's healthier. Anyway, did you see what happened at the end?"

"Yup."

"The nine o'clock news said that there had been some kind of earth tremor which caused the old mine workings to collapse. Mud slides, flooding...it's incredible."

"And did you believe all that, Cass?"

"Well something amazing obviously did happen," she said. "I suppose I was lucky to get out in time."

"It was Kerak's army, Cass. It was. I heard them singing. I saw them marching. This time they were not going to be defeated by the forces of evil. They were going to save the wild places, the trees, the plants, the animals...and it was them who pulled down their own ancient mining shafts and tunnels, it was them who caused the landslide. And it must have been that Water Goddess of yours, the Lady of the Lake or whatever she's called, who let the waters rip. It was wicked, Cass, wicked..."

"I do believe you Jay, you know I do. I saw them gathering in the cave of the Horned God. But didn't they do a lot of damage to the forest, too? So many trees were torn up."

"The trees will grow back. Nature heals its wounds very quickly."

"You're still the poet, Jay Cunningham." Cass flashed him a smile. "But – is it all over? How do we know that the contractors won't come back and start their work all over again?"

"Have you seen today's papers?" Jay slapped a rolled up copy onto the dinner table.

Cass opened it out. "I didn't have time to

look into the shop this morning. I was too busy trying to find all my old school stuff. And I was keeping clear of Mum."

Cass looked at the articles and the diagrams and the opinion column. Seismology was the problem, it seemed. There was one of those 'ology words from the appeal, again. What did it mean?

"Earthquake science!" laughed Jay, watching her frown. Cass read on. It seemed that yesterday's earth tremor had proved one scientific point that had been rejected at that appeal. The ground in this area really was unstable, likely to shift at any time. The engineers had been forced to change their minds and the accountants, seeing the costs of the project double and then treble, now changed their minds. This was not a suitable route for a motorway after all, it seemed...

"So do you think that's it, then?" asked Cass.

"Sounds like it to me."

Cass smiled and stretched.

"Well done, JC."

"You too, CD."

"Jay."

"Yes?"

"I think we should start a new campaign. To have the woods recognised officially as a nature reserve. So that it stays protected for all time."

"Don't you ever give up, Cass?" laughed Jay.

The bell rang for lessons.

Next Sunday the newspapers confirmed the good news, that the plans for the motorway link had been dropped.

In his front room, Ray Cunningham was reading the small ads. 'Caretaker wanted at Sheriton Secondary School.' Hmm, that one might be worth applying for. The pay wasn't too bad. If he got the job, he'd be able to keep a closer eye on that rascally son of his, too.

"What do you reckon my chances of getting this job would be?" he asked his wife as she came in from duty at the hospital.

Rose Cunningham looked for her reading glasses.

"Pretty good!" said Rose Cunningham. "We might just get that holiday next year after all!"

Lizzie Day was glad that the road had been cancelled. Now at last her daughter might start behaving like a normal human being again. If teenagers were ever capable of being human!

Lizzie was making a special meal for Phil Sergeant, who was telling her of his plans for leaving the police force in January. He thought she was looking quite interested. But Will was looking at the two of them suspiciously.

Mrs Bodgett was in church, convinced that it was her part in the protest that had done the trick. Mr Bodgett was by her side, and at his grumpiest. The congregation was singing a hymn, and Mrs Bodgett's voice soared above all the others, quavering on the highest notes:

"The golden evening brightens in the west;
Soon, soon to faithful warriors cometh rest;
Sweet is the calm of Paradise the blest..."

If Cass and Jay had heard the words of this hymn, it might well have made them think of Kerak.

But the two teenagers had walked up to Lookout Rock. This weekend had been fine and cold. As the sun dropped out of sight, yellow tongues of fire lit up wild tatters of purple cloud.

"What do you see, Jay?" asked Cass.

"I see Kerak's army of warriors marching off into the sun. Led by a prancing stag. Leaving the world to new people, to new beliefs..."

"Leaving the world to us, Jay." Cass looked at the darkening curve of the downs. A distant cheer floated on the air. "The warriors are being welcomed into paradise," she added.

"Who's the poet now?" laughed Jay. "That cheer came from the recreation ground, and you know it. Crickstone is playing football against Sheriton Town, this afternoon."

"We'd better catch the end of the game, then," said Cass.

Chapter 21
The Tomb Closes

The first snow of winter lay over the downs, drifting into great banks in the deep fold of Crickstone Woods. The trees, black against the white drifts, looked like stark, black skeletons.

The whole landscape lay still. The silence was broken only by the chatter of a small group of figures huddled by the mouth of a deep, dark shaft. They wore orange overalls and helmets and were piling up ropes, torches and other supplies.

For some weeks now the Sheriton cavers had been carrying out a new survey of the upper cave system beneath the downs. It was a risky business. After the earth tremor of the autumn, many tunnels had been blocked by falls of soil and rubble.

Exploring Cass' tunnel, as they called it, the cavers had come across the ancient carvings and mysterious rock paintings Cass had seen during her underground ordeal. Amazed, they had contacted the county archaeological trust. Linda Brookes, the director, now stood shivering by the carved spiral at the entrance to the underground world. It looked like the mouth of hell, she thought wryly. Not a hell of flames and burning sulphur, but a cold hell of ice and freezing black water. Icicles hung from the rock ledges.

Linda Brookes was more used to long digs in the open air, in the summer sun. Roman forts or watermills from the Middle Ages. She had never been underground before and was glad that this expedition was led by experienced cavers. She felt safe in their company.

Linda was startled when she first saw the bats clinging to the roof of the first cave. They were now hibernating, sleeping through the cold months of winter with their wings folded over their bodies. Sensible creatures. She wished she was tucked up in a warm bed herself right now.

Down she went, following the leader. Wading, swimming, squeezing. As they stretched up again, the caver waved leftwards at the rock wall. Lamp beams were raised towards the rock paintings. Linda gasped. These were the most remarkable examples she had seen outside France or Spain. The animal pictures tumbled across the stone and at the bottom was this extraordinary dancing figure, human yet wearing the antlers of a stag.

But the real surprise came when the expedition entered the great cave, the centre of all the tunnels and shafts marked on the spiral carving. There had been falls of rock here – very recent ones. And these had opened up a series of chambers which could now be seen in the crumbling cave wall. It looked to Linda as if they had been hacked out long ago, using primitive tools of stone and bone. She pulled a small trowel and a hand pick from her pack and began to scrape away at the rubble. The beam of light from her lamp pierced the gloom.

At first Linda thought her eyes were playing tricks on her. Could that be...surely not? A long thighbone was sticking out of the soil. And here were shells and stone beads, probably the remains of a necklace. With growing excitement she realised she had discovered something really incredible: a series of Stone Age burial chambers. With the remains of many bodies still lying there, undisturbed for thousands of years!

Linda knew she would have to come back later with experts. This was no time to disturb the site. But as she worked her way along one rock ledge, her torch picked out a sight that she was never to forget. A skeleton, probably that of a young girl, had sprawled out of one chamber, arms outstretched.

And opposite the cracked, bony hands was a skull. It had no body attached to it. Its dark, empty eye sockets seemed to be staring towards the skeleton. Now, this skull wasn't covered in soil stains. In fact it looked out of place, as if it had been put there very recently.

Linda frowned, puzzled. She began to crawl over towards the strange sight, when the leader of the cavers tapped her urgently on the shoulder. He pointed towards the shaft in the ceiling of the cave, through which they had rescued Cass. At first Linda thought it was snow floating down the tall, narrow chimney. She thought it looked rather beautiful. But then she realised that this was a shower of dust and soil. It was followed by a hail of small pebbles, which she could hear rattling down the cliff into the deep, icy water.

No panic! The team kept their cool and edged their way carefully towards the entrance of Cass' tunnel. Linda felt as if the earth was squeezing in on her, and began shaking in terror. She was pushed urgently and roughly into the dark passage.

No sooner had the team surfaced, their hearts beating wildly, than they heard a great roar behind them. The chimney had finally collapsed, filling the cave with slabs of stone and clumps of earth and ice. The tunnel behind them was blocked with a rock fall.

Linda and the cavers stared at each other without speaking as blackness closed in at last on the ancient world.

I am truly buried now, me and my people, sealed forever, deep inside the earth. My skull's last sight was of my sister, my sister from long ago, holding out her hands to me from the grave.

But Cass' spirit is free, for she lives again in the real world of flesh and blood, of life, love and pain. Shall I ever know that world again myself? It is not for me to decide. For now, while the remains of my body sleep, my spirit shall hunt the new sun across the stormy skies of winter.